Nihil

A Nivaari Novel, Volume 1

Charles M. Brown

Published by Charles Brown, 2024.

NIHIL

First edition. May 27, 2024.

ISBN: 979-8227756602

Written by Charles M. Brown.

Also by Charles M. Brown

A Nivaari Novel
Nihil

Exploits of the Hellhound-verse
Exploits of an Underpaid Supernatural Bartender

Second Sypher Wars
Gaeth's Redemption

Watch for more at https://www.hellhoundsrun.com/.

Table of Contents

Dedication:
The longest love letter a man can write to the most amazing
woman in his life. None of this would ever be possible
without her.

Trigger Warning:
This book includes graphic scenes that may be disturbing to anyone who has worked Law Enforcement, EMS, or Fire. We've all worked bad scenes.
Any relation or representation to anyone living or dead, or to any entity or business are entirely fictional. Some geographic areas are mentioned, but the situations and story surrounding these events are fictional as well.

Prologue

Blue lights strobed into the cloud filled night. The wind was like icy fingers clawing at his spine seeking to rob him of every bit of warmth he had ever felt. A Deputy Sheriff rolls up on a vehicle overturned on the recently paved black top of Highway 421. A crumpled and mangled red minivan is upside down and had slid a good ways along the asphalt; leaving gouges in the black roadway for twenty feet. The van is still rocking slightly from its recent feat of automotive gymnastics. As the deputy approaches, some part of his mind notices the rear half of the vehicle looks almost brand new. The red paint, still crisp in the bright lights from the cruiser. The front half, however, is just gone. There is no front end left, like an angry giant had ripped off the front axle and engine compartment and tossed it into the night. As the Deputy exits his patrol car he can hear a man and woman screaming. Though screaming was not a strong enough word for the gut-wrenching, soul tearing, sound being uttered by the occupants of the vehicle. Howling like the lost souls of the damned forever banished from the light. It caused the deputy to feel more than the icy cold running up his spine. The cold of fear, of apprehension, at what he had stumbled upon filled his soul. The deputy runs to the van to find a man and woman in the front seats and a teenage boy in the middle rear of the van. All three are still held in place, upside down, by seat belts. It's a surreal site with their hair hanging straight down towards the roof of the cab. The complete perspective change from the deputies' own is disorienting.

The adults were screaming so much the deputy couldn't actually hear what they were trying to say. The teenager in the back was silent. Unconscious or dead from the crash. The deputy couldn't tell. The wails were unintelligible and somehow seemed both loud and just a little bit far away. Small and tiny like the telephone game children play with cans and a string. The deputy yanks on the driver side door, fighting the warped and asphalt scraped metal to try to get to the family. As the Deputy strains against the door, he sees a white shape flop to the ground. Suddenly everything is red. Everything is turning red and the deputy feels warm wetness strike his face. He tastes a coppery liquid coat on his tongue. The deputy somehow realizes that the driver's arm has been severed in the accident. It had fallen to the ground, limp dead meat, as the deputy tried to free the driver. The deputy scrambles as the taste of copper fills his mouth. He was trained for this he keeps screaming inwardly. The tourniquet goes around the stump and is then pulled tight. As the deputy tightens the little stick on top of the tourniquet the driver blacks out from blood loss and pain. That was a blessing for both the driver and the deputy. It tore the deputies soul to hurt someone who he was trying to save but tourniquets are not comfortable devices to have applied. They cause a great deal of pain to the patient while trying to save the patient's life. The deputy knew that, but it was still a bad moment in a string of horrific ones.

The deputy looks around trying to understand where his help is. Where was EMS and Fire? He knew they were coming, they always came. Where was his zone partner? It was at that moment that the deputy saw her, or what was left of her. Reality snaps into focus all at once. The woman is screaming, "my daughter, my daughter". And he sees it, sees her. Approximately 20 feet in front of the van is a small, huddled form all bundled in white. A child's form lay lax and lifeless, but not whole. A few feet further along the icy black top rests a small head facing the deputy. Just sitting there, not a scratch on the translucent skin, but appearing as though it was just waiting patiently for the deputy to notice. Beautiful blond hair and clear striking blue eyes staring at the deputy. Like the head was still alive and the girl was trying to tell him something. It felt as though that gaze would convey the sadness of the entire world if he continued to look into her eyes. The deputy felt a sudden sense of vertigo. His head swam and confusion raced through his mind. He felt as though he were both in his body looking at the child's severed head, and seeing himself from the ground from far away, as if he were looking at himself through the clear blue eyes of the baby girl who would never grow up. Never grow older, never know sadness or joy. Never see her prom or have her heart broke or watch her own children be born and grow up. The deputy vomited profusely like a great angry volcano spewing in every direction. It was with this intense vertigo and feeling his body void its entire contents at once that he watched the pavement rise to meet him as he passed out.

Blessed blackness claimed his mind and soul, hopefully to protect his psyche from any further mind destroying trauma.

Chapter One

I woke up drenched in sweat and gasping. A scream clawing at the back of my throat. My heart felt like it was about to break my sternum trying to escape my chest. The dream of that night is always the same. Reliving the tragedy that drove me out of law enforcement. Reliving the moment that cost me my home and marriage. In the dreams it's worse. Sometimes the little girl is screaming or begging for her mommy or demanding to know why I didn't save her. The guilt and grief of that night haunts my dreams. Who am I kidding? It haunts my dreams every night. Sometimes I think her ghost haunts me because she blames me for not getting there in time. Or maybe I just blame myself. I mean, there's no such thing as ghosts, right?

Slowly, I started coming out of the dream and back to reality. My parents named me Cygnus Magnus but I go by Cy. My folks claimed it was a long held family tradition given only to children born every few generations. They said it meant I was destined for greatness. I thought it sounded like a Monty Python skit but I would have never told them that. I mean I'm sure my parents felt very strongly about the name but I had to learn to fight way before I should have just to defend my school yard honor. My folks were amazing parents who did the best they could; so it could have been worse. My grandfather's name was Evelyn Cyril, so yeah, it could have been much worse.

I stared up at the yellowed ceiling trying to calm my breathing, my legs tangled in the plaid dime store sheets. I'd lived alone since the divorce. I missed my ex-wife but I understood why she had to leave. She had to go on with her life. We had fallen out of love a long time ago. After leaving law enforcement I didn't know which way was up. I was lost in a world I didn't understand. That was just too much strain on a marriage already on the rocks. Like so many, we had just become different people and were heading in different directions. Not her fault at all, I truly wanted her to succeed and be happy and she couldn't do that with me.

I stumbled groggily to the bedroom, almost falling on my face. It was a horrible little apartment. The walls and ceiling were stained with old water damage and who knew what else. Every wall was yellowed and dingy from years of hate and nicotine. A black light and some luminol would probably give a forensic team a heart attack. Better not to know. The sink was chipped and stained, and the toilet probably had its own sentient colony of bacteria. Looking into the cracked mirror was always a bit startling now. Red hair, red beard and green eyes staring back at me. Gold hoops in my left ear and full sleeves tattooed along my arms added to the sight of just how much I'd changed. Standing six foot two and with the rib cage, shoulders and arms of someone six foot five, finding a dress shirt was challenging, but I was hell on the weight pile or in a street fight. What no one noticed was that I could also read and even conjugate.

The sickly yellow light of the overhead glared angrily around the room which just added to the feeling that the entire apartment couldn't be made clean with a flame thrower and holy water. Maybe thermite or a small yield nuke? I wasn't even sure that would work honestly. It was the kind of place where the cockroaches had street names and threw gang signs when you tried to kill them.

After freshening up in the bathroom and hoping that I didn't need a tetanus booster I made my way into the little kitchenette. A dented stove and an even more worn dinette table filled most of the tiny area. Blearily I worked my way to my beloved coffee pot. If a dog is man's best friend, coffee is proof that somewhere there is a divine intelligence that loves us.

With the first warm bitterness renewing my flagging will to live I got dressed for the day. Going from being a well-paid Sergeant in the local Sheriff's Office to being an underpaid pizza boy was a rough transition. Not mentally, though I missed my team and my friends, but more financially. There were a lot of nights where my only sustenance was left over pizza the store was going to throw out. There were lots of other jobs I could have had immediately. Good money, benefits, travel. But I'd have to put on the badge again. Or at least some form of it. I just wasn't ready yet. Since no one was hiring ex-cops and combat medics for jobs in the civilian world, I took a job delivering pizzas. It's not good work, but it's an honest job and I'm not taking money from the government to survive. My grandfather, the aforementioned Evylyn Cyril, had survived the Great Depression and I always remembered what he said, "pride don't fill bellies, boy". He was exactly right.

Jeans, tactical boots size fourteen extra wide thank you, and a hoodie were uniform of the day. I always kept a Glock 43 I'd custom built in an inner pants holster; as well as my folding knife, flashlight and the gris gris my grandma had given me before she died. A gris gris is a bag, usually red velvet, containing different herbs and charms. They can be custom made for luck, money, love, protection, or other uses. I'm not sure if it helps or not but it's just something I've carried since I first started having fuzz on my chin, or other places. Old habits are hard to break. Besides, I could use good luck. I'd been on a bad run for a long time. A really long time.

The night seemed like any other. Some good tips, some folks who should have gone and got their own food. Always tip your delivery driver, folks, because they are completely alone with your food for long periods of time. And they have a knack for remembering who doesn't tip. Just saying.

At around one in the morning a delivery came through for a newer neighborhood in the suburbs of Winston. Nothing new there, people were always ordering in the middle of the night. I just had to watch out for robbers or punk kids wanting to play bash the pizza boy. It's funny how my new job paid a lot less than my old one and yet the risks of getting shot were pretty much the same. I grabbed my pizza bag and headed out. The entire drive didn't take more than eight minutes, but I just couldn't shake this nebulous feeling of doom. Like I used to feel knowing I was walking into an ambush. But it was a pizza not a warrant, so I turned up the music and drove on.

Turning down Baxter St. I kept looking for the address while jamming out to old school metal. The night seemed darker the further I went down the road. As I continued on I suddenly ran out of mailboxes. Generally, no mailbox at night means no address to easily find. The road kept going but the houses and street lights just stopped. My imagination pictured an unholy DMZ between the rest of the neighborhood and whatever lay ahead. The area was poorly lit to begin with but here, at what seemed like the end of the road, it was darker. It wasn't just a lack of streetlights, it was as if there was a thread of oppression and dread in the breathing darkness of the night. I had the fleeting worry that the "end of the road", so to speak, might be just that.

The paved road had turned to a gravel path. I shook it off and started down the gravel drive. When I began this delivery I was hoping the customer would tip but now I was just worried about staying safe. There was a wrongness to this that I could not understand.

It's funny but I didn't remember Baxter St. going this far back. I knew I'd delivered out here probably fifty times, but I didn't remember ever going this far. Just as I was about to say screw it and turn around, I saw an old dented gray mailbox half propped up on a thick pine tree. Shining my flashlight on the side of the old dented metal mailbox I could just make out the address I was looking for. It was painted on the metal like some dyslexic arachnid with pretentions had been set loose on the thing. Hopping back in my car I proceeded down the worn rutted path of a driveway. The trees were all overgrown going down the drive and the branches felt like they were reaching out and trying to claw at the car. As if the trees were angry that I was invading their territory by driving down the gravel path. The potholes in the worn gravel road made me think of greedy mouths lurking to devour any traveler foolish enough to pass this way. All in all, I did not have a happy feeling about this.

After off roading for about a quarter mile I could just see a faint porch light ahead. It was dim and difficult to make out. The darkness swarmed around the faint glow. I had the thought that the darkness was trying to devour the light like it was a mortal enemy. I realized I couldn't even see the outline of the house. All I could see was the front porch. The porch was old, rotten and looked like something I would fall right through as soon as I stepped on it. The porch light was about as effective as a guttering candle and barely illuminated a brown wood door I assumed to be as rotten as the porch. This had to be a prank. No way was anyone living in this dilapidated rat hole. I mean, no offense to honest rats, but this place looked like it was condemned thirty years ago and someone was squatting in it. My happy meter was pegging negative one thousand as I got out of my car and gently touched my Glock in case I suddenly needed it. Yes, I know we're not supposed to carry guns on deliveries. Yes, I know it's a violation of corporate policy. And yes, you should know I'm not dying delivering some damn fool pizza. Two dollars an hour plus tips isn't worth my life.

As I reached into the back seat to get my bag every single hair on my body suddenly stood up. And let me tell you, when even your pubic hair stands at attention, it's a trifle disconcerting. Every cell in my body was awake with that quiet surety that I was about to be fired upon and return fire. I knew as sure as I knew my name that something was about to happen. But this was crazy. I wasn't in a war zone, and I wasn't on a hot call. I was delivering a pizza to a scary old house. As this thought bumped through my mind, I noticed a putrid smell. Something so foul you knew you would be smelling it for days and wanting to vomit the entire time. The smell reminded me of a suicide I had worked one August when I was a rookie. A farmer had found a car in the middle of a field. He called us because he just didn't feel right about it. I had to bang on the window to knock the maggots off the inside of the glass so that I could see the body. And when we opened the door? Yeah, that smell.

I started to approach the door of the house when I noticed the air just felt heavy. It was hard to breath with some unknown lurking pressure giving the air an anxiety inducing weight and substance. As if it were alive and didn't want me there. Add to that the entire area was utterly silent. No bats, no crickets, not even the wind moving through the clawing branches of the trees that were looming over me. I felt like I was in a sinister cave formed by a canopy of ancient whispering pines and oaks that filled every part of the property. I secured the pizza bag in my left hand and started walking to the door. Weird optical illusions seemed to cause the shadows to writhe and play at the edges of the flashlight's beam, making it look like the dark was a living thing. And that living thing was, in turn, hungry to devour the light. A demented yin and yang.

I gingerly stepped up onto the rotten, almost desiccated, front porch and prayed a silent prayer to The Great Lord Tipus, the god of all delivery drivers, that I would not fall through the porch. The feeling of being watched played through me again, reigniting that certainty that something bad was about to happen. This whole situation was as weird as a three peckered billy-goat.

I knocked and the door echoed hollowly through the house. I wondered if this was what beating on the door to an ancient mausoleum might sound like. I was in the process of seriously considering leaving the food on the doorstep and high tailing it back to my car but I knocked a second time. Sometimes I'm not the smartest child my parents gifted to the world.

"Just a minute", called a thin reedy female voice through the door.

"If the door creaks open and the crypt keeper answers I'm unloading my Glock in his nuts", I whispered under my breath in disgust.

The door creaked inward until I could see an elderly pale female in one of those motorized scooters. The skin of her face was gray like old ash and she had wispy white hair. High cheekbones with round eyes and a short pointed nose framed a thin lipped mouth. Her mouth seemed a little too wide for her face. The old lady's eyes were dark orbs as she looked at me. I couldn't seem to focus on any one detail about her for very long. My mind just seemed to skitter over the details while trying to accept the entirety of the scene. She was wearing a nasty white blouse with a pale blue throw over her legs and had a black cane that was clutched in her left hand. Her fingers seemed too long for her hands with dark yellow nails like small talons protruding from her fingertips.

"CJ's Pizza ma'am, got your order hot and fresh right here", I said, flashing my best customer service smile. Smiling service and hot food and never you mind that I was seriously freaked by the whole encounter. Nope, Captain Customer Service, that's me. Besides, I already knew I wasn't getting a tip. At this point I just wanted to escape without being sacrificed in some pagan ritual.

"Oh, thank you, young man", the old lady said, reminding me of about a thousand horror movies with that breathy high-pitched voice. "Can you bring it in the kitchen", she asked. "My legs don't work so well anymore", she said and chortled. Her laugh was of the kind that you knew there was a joke and you really didn't want to know what it was.

Without thinking I started into the house. I entered a long dirt strewn hallway with scarred wooden floors and gray wallpaper along the walls. There were cobwebs all along the ceiling and the air smelled of dust and decay. That smell of stale air when a place has been empty for a long time. I could see the kitchen straight ahead at the end of the hall. The kitchen had a single overhead light glowing weakly in the gloom of the house. It barely lit the baby puke green walls and the damaged wooden cabinets with their doors hanging crooked in the weak light.

Three steps into the house the word, "Stop", screamed through my mind. It went through every atom of my being like lightning. My entire soul was silent and my breathing paused as though it were afraid to leave my lungs. I knew, in that moment, that if I took one more step into that house I was going to die!

It was silent, the entire house was silent. Not a whirring fan, a tv, a cat scuttling through the house. It wasn't an absence of sound but rather that there was absolutely no sound at all. I looked to my right and into the living room. I'm not sure why but I suffered a compulsion to look that way. On the couch was a mountain of old dolls. Baby dolls, Barbies, stuffed dolls all mounded around a single Raggedy Ann doll sitting on the couch. It occurred to me that the Raggedy Ann doll was holding court over all the other dolls on the couch.

Just as my eyes made sense of what I was seeing the Raggedy Ann doll moved. It friggin' moved all on its own. It turned its head to stare directly at me and what I thought were black button eyes were actually black burning sentient orbs in the stained white cloth face. Its red curly hair crackled around its face and its small sewn hands clutched at the wrinkled white apron. I felt like the doll was peering through my flesh and judging the weight of my soul. I wanted to weep at the wave of sorrow and misery that seemed to emanate from the gaze of that lonely doll.

"Is something wrong dear", the old lady asked. I snapped my gaze back to her as she spoke. She had been backing her motorized wheelchair down the hall towards the kitchen but had stopped when I had.

"Ma'am, I'm so sorry, I forgot that a new policy came out that drivers aren't supposed to go into people's homes anymore. I really do apologize", I stammered while trying to sound suave and unintimidated.

I couldn't make out her face. I thought I saw it clearly when she first came to the door but now, I wasn't sure of anything. It was still just so quiet. The crippled old lady slowly began to stand up from her chair.

"You're going to come in dear", she said. Her voice was getting deeper and resonated off the walls as she rose from the chair. Dust and cobwebs began shaking from the ceiling down on both of us. "I'm so hungry", she roared in a voice gone so deep I felt it rattling in my chest.

As her voice bounced and hissed, shadows wormed and crawled down the walls, coalescing at her feet like thick ropey maggots. The walls which had seemed normal at first, were now rotted with wallpaper hanging in ribbons from the ancient plaster. The shadows coiled and writhed in a putrid feast of worship around the old lady's lower legs as she stood and continued to grow. Looking into her face I could see that her eyes had grown to the size of golf balls and were as pitch black as those of the Raggedy Ann doll. Her wispy white hair was suddenly just strands hanging loosely from her putrefied scalp. Her eyes continued to grow and her nose seemed to have rotted off, leaving her sinus cavity exposed like a leper.

Seeing her teeth reminded me of stories of old mutant cannibals. They were all gleaming yellow sharpened points in what was now a black slash of a mouth which stretched from ear to ear. Her blouse was ripped and her breasts were large and gray hanging past her navel. As she raised both arms to point at me, pustules exploded from around her right nipple. Black ooze squirted into the writhing shadows on the floor.

"Come here", she bellowed as she pointed those razor-like claws in my direction.

I couldn't process this. What was I seeing? What was happening? I froze. I've never frozen but this situation was outside any training or experience I had ever had. My conscious mind demanded to make sense of this but my caveman brain wanted to run for the hills. Strangely I could feel a burning in my left-hand pocket. Suddenly, my thigh and groin were cooking like meat on a grill at a July Fourth barbeque. Blue green flames were shooting out of my pocket. Slapping at my leg and yelping in outrage I tried to save my testicles from becoming roasted nuts.

I reached into my pocket and yanked out the burning item to discover that it was my gris gris. It was engulfing my hand in blue flame but wasn't burning me now that I held it out in the open. The flames seemed to be coalescing into patterns around my hand before collapsing and reforming into new ones. I fell to my knees, my whole body weak with shock, and my mind reeling from the sudden failure of reality.

Looking up I saw the shadows slithering along the floor towards me. As the old lady took her first thundering step towards me, the ropey shadow maggots began to surround me. Desperately searching for any kind of weapon I felt something round on the floor hidden by the foul shadows. Grasping it as the creature lumbered towards me, I realized that the round object was a broken wooden mop handle. The monster wrapped her pustulent fingers around my skull and I gagged from the gangrenous smell of her flesh. Its left breast smacked me in the face leaving a stain of black ichor dripping down my chin. I wanted to wretch from the smell but I knew if I opened my mouth that rot would invade my body. I wrapped the hand that held the gris gris around the mop handle and brought the sharpened stake up into the creature's chest just under the sternum and through where its black slimy heart should have been. The improvised stake was burning through the creature, the fire surrounding the stake flashing green and blue. I could smell the creature's rotten flesh cooking in a bitter choking miasma of dead corpses and rotting intestines.

"I'll kill you, you bastard, I'll kill you and eat your soul", the creature shrieked.

The thunder of the creature's voice made my whole body vibrate from its bass. Black puss and coagulated blood spewed forth from the creature and covered my face and neck making my eyes water and my stomach churn with the need to vomit everything I had ever eaten up in that moment. The stench was so horrific it felt like my soul was tainted with it. Have you ever smelled something so bad you thought maggots would run from it? I wasn't just smelling it, I was tasting it.

The snaking shadows writhed and climbed up our entwined bodies as though they would devour us both. The creature was clawing and bellowing, and I was driving that stake up and through with muscles I didn't know my body had. My arms were spasming, the braided muscles of my forearms clenching under my tattooed skin as I pushed the stake through the creature's back. The flames surrounding the improvised weapon went from bluish green to a harsh deep red. If you gave hate a color it would be that shade of red. The flames felt intelligent in that moment and, moreover, they were pissed off like a drill instructor whose boots just got scuffed. The flames consumed the hideous beast and, with an intense popping sound, the beast imploded. It sprayed thick chunks of meat and rotten juices throughout the hallway. All that remained was a gentle vacuum sucking fetid air for a moment before fading away.

I collapsed onto the floor retching and gasping for air. My entire body felt like I had just tried to lift an elephant and my vision was graying out. I laid on the ground feeling like a guppy out of water for a few minutes before I started to regain my senses. Vision slowly returning, I dug around on the floor for my flashlight. The creature and the writhing maggot shadows were gone. And so were the lights on the porch and in the kitchen. I was in a rotten abandoned house. The air had that deep funk of mold that you could feel invading your lungs on every breath. The plaster on the walls was mostly busted out with a few pieces held together by bits of rotting wall paper. The house suddenly had the vibe of a place long disused and abandoned but without the soul crushing evil stain which had marred it just a moment before.

Sensing movement I turned towards the living room archway to see a shambling Raggedy Ann doll approaching me. In the weak beam of my flashlight it seemed as though the doll's stitches were unraveling. Holding out one small white cloth hand in an imploring gesture I clearly heard the soft words, "thank you", before the doll dissolved into a pile of rags. And the strangest thing? The doll's eyes, in that last moment, had been a vibrant green. A child's eyes in a doll's face.

Chapter Two

S itting in the rear of the Bus, the affectionate term for an ambulance, I had a blanket draped over my shoulders and sat with an oxygen mask draped loosely over my nose and mouth. I had a nice four-inch gash above my left eye, but it had stopped bleeding. Well, it had mostly stopped bleeding anyway. I had convinced the cute female EMT, Perkins, to stitch up the wound on my head in the back of the Bus instead of transporting me to the hospital. It was a big no no, and something she shouldn't be doing, but I'm sure my winning smile helped. Either that or the large African American Lieutenant standing just outside who had asked her very sweetly to help me out before turning back to me and providing me a world class ass chewing for stupidity and just breathing. Honestly I kind of thought she was just enjoying the impressive flowing invective aimed in my direction. The lieutenant was actually my former Field Training Officer in the Sheriff's Office and a very good friend. He had brought me up from an idiot rookie to an almost good cop. Lt. Sam Clark stood six foot four with muscles for days. Dressed in a navy blue check pattern suit jacket, navy slacks, a pale Carolina blue button up shirt and missing his tie, he was the epitome of well-dressed and dapper. Handsome devil too. Back in the day, before I married, I used to marvel at how the women used to throw themselves at him. Not much had changed on that score but he was always faithful to his wife. He would just chuckle and point to his ring. They usually took the disappointment well. No criticism there, we used to back each other up on that. While I was married I did the same thing. You either did the right thing or you got divorced, it was that simple.

EMT Perkins wouldn't tell me her first name, but I sure did appreciate the gentle floral smell of her perfume, or maybe it was just fabric softener, and her black hair tied up in a messy bun. Look, I was single and it had been a while ok? I tried convincing her that if she was going to sew up my head then she had an ethical obligation to check on my health and well being after her shift but she wasn't buying. She did have a nice smile though. I grimaced as she took the mask from me and started dragging the metal fiber through the skin of my brow, neatly pulling the flesh closed.

"So, what the hell happened in there Cy", Sam demanded hotly.

"How the hell should I know", I retorted. "I was delivering a pizza and got hit on the head", I said pointing at the now half-sewn gash in my skull as evidence.

"Hold still or this will be crooked", Perkins said and swatted me. I really wasn't sure if I was ready to date again but she did have me considering the prospect. A strong woman who can stitch wounds is harder to find than gold. Forget the cooking stereotype, medic skills are where it's at.

"Damnit Cy, there's no way that's all that happened", Sam said, "when we were in SWAT I saw you drop suspects no one else would go near with one hit. There's no way some punk got the drop on you", he continued with an angry fire gleaming in his eyes.

Sam knew I was lying. We'd been partners and friends for over twenty years. He knew when I was full of shit and had no problem calling me on it. He knew what I could do and just how good I was at it. Hell, he had been my ring man for several MMA bouts I did just for fun. If I had more time I would have said I tripped and fell. But, somehow, I knew he wouldn't have believed that either.

"Look Lieutenant", I started hotly and then sighed and slowed down. It wasn't his fault I'd just tripped through the twilight zone. It wasn't his fault that I was scared and freaking out and couldn't admit why. "Sam, I'm sorry, I'm just not sure. I got my bell rung pretty good and it's just kind of a blur. I'm sorry", I said again with a little frustration in my voice. I hated lying to my friend. I really did, but how was I supposed to admit what had just happened. I didn't even believe it and I was there.

Sam looked at me for a minute, all righteous anger, and then shook his head and chuckled softly, "Kind of like when that little Latina girl rung your bell with a frying pan back when you were a rookie", Sam asked evilly. That one call had been an embarrassment my entire career. She had split my head wide open with a pan full of bacon. Bacon mind you. Sam knew I was sensitive about it and chose to rib me for the many years of our friendship when he wanted to push my buttons. I didn't mind that she had knocked me out. Women are just as much warriors as men. I minded that it was a pan full of bacon. Cop, pan full of bacon, you get the joke. I never lived that one down.

"Do women beat you up a lot Cy", Perkins asked. Her voice was soft with a little huskiness in it. Damn, but she was sexy. And, hey, she knew my name. The night was looking up.

"Only if that's what you're into", I said, glancing at her playfully. I grinned roguishly at her. She gave a sharp jerk to the last stitch and I may have yelped a little. She chuckled in true sadistic fashion. Sam began laughing so hard it drew the stares of the responding officers who were standing by gossiping until the LT told them they could clear the scene. It had to be a strange sight for them. The uber professional Lieutenant Clark, laughing like a human being. Unheard of!

"Come on Romeo", Sam said while motioning for me to get out of the Bus. "I think you're wasting your time on this one", he said, smiling at Perkins.

As I got out of the bus Perkins turned to Sam and said, "he is Lieutenant, but you wouldn't be", while looking Sam up and down in a meaningful fashion.

"Perkins", Sam said seriously, "my wife would kill me and probably try and run off with you just for the life insurance. No thanks", he said firmly, holding his hands up in front of him in a stern but comical gesture.

Perkins smiled delightedly and said, "I might be up for that too", then laughed and shut the double doors.

"I can't take you anywhere", I said to Sam. "I mean, seriously, I know you're better looking and have better suits but what do you have that I don't", I jokingly complained.

Sam knew I was kidding, he knew how much my divorce had messed with my head. But he went along with the joking.

"Hey", Sam said, "it's not my fault you dress like a drunk biker. If you'd dress like a grown up you might get treated like one". He was referring to the beard, earrings, and penchant for leather I had developed since leaving law enforcement. He really had no appreciation for taste or the well matched hoodie to jeans color scheme of my wardrobe.

"Well", I replied, "I didn't want to look like a cop anymore."

Sam became suddenly serious, "it wasn't your fault Cy. You found them. You saved them. The parents even said you were the reason the rest of the family was alive at all". Sam grabbed me by the shoulders and looked me in the eyes, "you did everything you could. You did more than anyone else would have known to do. It's time to stop. It's time to let it go".

"Thanks", I said and shook him off. I paused and took a deep breath before continuing. "I know you're right", another pause and then I shook my head and tried again, "I know you're right. I'm just not the same guy anymore. I'm just not". The guilt of not being able to do more that night still tore at me. Still left an unhealed crater in my soul. I was one of the better medics ever to survive Special Forces Selection. I had more experience than most civilian doctors. But I couldn't save them. Not that night and not my night since then in my nightmares.

"Let's go talk to Detective Fields so we can get everyone back on the road", Sam said and sighed. He sounded defeated, like I was disappointing him. I probably was. We had been through a lot together. We'd seen hundreds of calls, went to SWAT school together, fought together, drank together, hell he'd been my best man at my wedding. He wasn't a friend. He was the closest thing I'd had to family for years. And I knew he felt my pain like it was his own. But I couldn't let it go. I just didn't know how to set the weight of it down yet.

We walked carefully back down the rutted driveway to where my rusted out vehicle sat. I noticed the night no longer felt oppressive and the trees seemed like normal trees now. They no longer clawed at the air like monsters craving to devour human flesh. Even the headlights on my car seemed to be brighter than when I had first arrived.

Detective Clara Fields stood in front of my beater writing furiously in her handy dandy field notebook and shivering in her smart, but off the rack, gray pants suit. With her café colored skin she really needed to get Sam to take her shopping. Or Sam's wife, to be honest. I tried to bribe Sam's wife Betty many times to admit she was the one who picked out Sam's clothes but she would just smile and ignore me. The pants suit did nothing to show off Clara's natural beauty or the curves of her body. But I always pretended not to notice. I had trained Clara as a detective when she was still green and that made her persona non nookie.

"Cy, what the hell happened here and why am I out here freezing my buns off", Clara demanded. Spinning to face me she pointed her ink pen at me and continued accusingly, "and further, if someone jumped you, where are all the bodies", she wanted to know. "The last person to swing on you had his jaw wired shut for six months and you slapped his eye clean out of the socket", she said and shuddered remembering the junkie who had swung on me after stabbing his girlfriend in the neck. It had been her first real violent incident and I don't think she ever forgave me for having to stabilize the guy's eyeball in her hands as EMS took him to the hospital.

"Why doesn't anyone believe me," I asked rhetorically. Both Sam and Clara just stared at me like I was stupid. I had to think fast to try and distract them both.

"You should be grateful", I said, "I probably saved your life that night".

"Grateful", she scoffed, folding her arms. "I still have nightmares about dangling eyeballs".

"You just need someone to cuddle up with and make you dream of other things", I said sweetly while grinning at her. If I could needle Clara I could probably keep her from asking too many questions. I hoped so anyway. I hated to lie to these two but what was I going to say? The Baba Yaga of Winston had tried to eat my soul? I'd be in a rubber room before nightfall. I didn't believe me, so how could they? Clara slapped me in the chest and made a groan of frustration before covering her face with her hands. She was blushing. No shit, she was actually blushing.

"Oh, who is he", I chortled, "or she for that matter. You know I think loving is an equal opportunity affair", I said, crowing slightly. Clara worked so hard to be a professional I always worried she'd forget to be human. I didn't want to see her fall into the same trap that so many of us did. I kind of looked at Clara as a kid sister and wanted the best for her.

"I don't know what the hell you're talking about", she stated flatly, but I could tell she was trying not to smile. She knew I cared about her and wanted her to be happy. But she was also a cop and we're a merciless sort given a good bit of gossip.

"Are you two about done", Sam asked while trying to glower menacingly and failing. He was having trouble holding back his smile.

Clara looked at Sam and said, "sorry, Lieutenant", at the same time I said, "she started it", in my best grown up voice.

"Cy, stop being a pain in the ass please", Sam said. He then looked at Clara and asked, "what have you got?" Sam was suddenly all business.

Clara straightened her back and put on her cop face. "Nothing, sir. No tire tracks, no footprints, no weapons left behind. K9 couldn't get a scent for the dog to track. Uniforms canvassed the area and couldn't find anything. Basically, Cy was attacked by a ninja or a ghost."

I stiffened at the ghost comment and Clara noticed but didn't say anything. "Unless Cy can give us something to go on, there are no leads to develop".

Both Sam and Clara looked at me and I tried not to look at my feet. "Guys, I'm sorry but I'll say it again, I took a hard hit, everything is still a blur." I could tell neither believed me, but they weren't going to press it either.

"Well if there's nothing else, we'll do the report and close it for now", Sam said and sighed. Sam looked at me and said, "if you remember anything you know what to do."

"Yep I do", I said and tried not to let them see me relax too much. Sam and Clara were both good cops and they already smelled something rotten. And it wasn't the anchovies. I had to be very careful with what I said until I could figure this out. I didn't like holding anything back, but I had no idea how to explain what had happened either.

Sam started to walk off to tell everyone to clear the scene, then stopped and looked back at me. "Cy, Betty wants you to come to dinner soon. But for fuck's sake take a shower and loose the earrings. You look like the MC version of Peter Pan", he shook his head and walked off.

Clara tried to hold it in but was overwhelmed with a giggling fit as Sam walked off. "Go ahead", I said to her in mock disgust, "before you hurt yourself".

Clara began howling with laughter, holding her sides and gasping. "You really do", she said, glancing at me. "Cy, I miss you, but don't you think your rebellion phase should have ended a long time ago? I mean, what are you rebelling against anyway", she asked.

"What have you got", I asked, looking at her seriously for a minute before we both couldn't hold the laughter in any longer. Brando I definitely was not, but it felt good to laugh and be among my own people again.

As the laughter faded Clara stepped up beside me and bumped me with her shoulder. "Are you ok, I mean, really ok", she asked earnestly.

"I think so", I said honestly. "I'm working on being ok, that's about the best I can do".

"You could come back you know", Clara said in a rush. "Everyone understands and respects you. They'd probably bring you back with full rank if you wanted".

I let that sit for a minute before replying softly, "no hon, not me. Thanks, but that part of my life is done. I love all of you but it's time to move on to better things girl".

"And are you, moving on to better things I mean". She asked, nudging me with her shoulder.

"What, you don't think a brilliant career in pizza delivery is a stellar move", I demanded jokingly while holding out both arms in a grandiose gesture.

She laughed and sighed all in the same breath. "Go home Cy and try to stay out of trouble", she said before walking back up the gravel drive to her car.

I decided this was good advice and went to get in my car. Looking around the area one last time I couldn't figure out what happened. I knew what I saw. I knew what I experienced. But how was any of this possible? Had someone slipped something in my coffee? Had I finally slipped my gears and needed the good old rubber room? Was any of it real? I just didn't know.

Chapter Three

Returning to my apartment I trudged up the rusted metal stairs to the second floor and walked down the darkened hall to my door. The vinyl siding in the hallway had started falling off the wall like dominoes and the hall ceiling had huge holes where the plaster had fallen out in clumps. The overhead light in the hall was out again leaving the walkway dark and vaguely threatening. In this neighborhood you never knew if it was the landlord failing to repair things like this or if the tenants broke it so they could continue with their business unobserved. It didn't pay to notice things too close here.

I felt too tired to put the key in the deadbolt and stood in front of the door for a minute just looking at the key dumbly. The wind screamed through the second floor hallway and the sudden temperature drop brought me back into the moment. The breeze was so strong I thought it would blow me off my feet. The wind carried with it a shrieking sound akin to what I thought the wailing dead trapped in Sheol might sound like. Could tonight really get any weirder? I was so tired and my body hurt everywhere. All I wanted was a hot shower, a shot of rye, and my lumpy mattress.

I opened the door and shambled inside my dark little apartment while trying not to trip on my own two feet. As I closed the door I noticed a faint light on in the kitchenette. I never leave lights on inside the apartment. As I cautiously stepped away from the door I thought maybe I had just forgotten to shut it off. It had been a weird night so it was possible. Attempting to move noiselessly on the stained brown carpet I smelled mothballs and something else. It smelled like someone had hidden rotten meat in grandma's closet. Having already had a night straight out of a horror novel I was in no mood to take chances. I drew my Glock 43 and brought the pistol up in the direction of the kitchen. As I pied the entryway I saw a figure dressed all in black sitting at the dinette table with its back to me. I made sure the front sight of my pistol rested squarely mid back just to the left of the spine. "Front sight in a fight", they had screamed at us over and over during combat pistol training.

"Shoot me, Mr. Magnus, and you will never understand what happened tonight", a gravel voice said. The figure did not move or even seem to breathe as it continued, "Shoot me, and you will be dead by moon rise". The stygian shrouded figure's voice was masculine and raspy as if he hadn't spoken in a very long time. I half expected a dust cloud to rise from the figure when he spoke, as if he had sat there for centuries waiting for me to arrive.

"Mister", I said, "I don't think you're in a position to threaten me right now. I have no problem emptying this mag in you". I was dead serious, no pun intended. I had taken all of the slack out of the trigger. A hard breath would have released the sear and sent 126 grains of burning badness into the body of the intruder.

"Mr. Magnus", the shrouded form said, "come here and sit down. We have much to discuss and I do not cherish the wasted sands of the hour glass."

"Wasted sands of the hour glass", I parroted back in a mocking tone. "Who the hell talks like that", I asked. This conversation was surreal at its mildest. I had a gun pointed at the back of the figure's heart. I was scared and I was going to live. Whether this damn fool did or not was debatable, but I was going to.

My arm was starting to get tired. Holding a shooting stance perfectly over time is an impossibility. I either needed to shoot or lower my weapon. Other than breaking into my apartment and being creepy as hell the figure had not acted threateningly. Yeah, not threatening at all really. That little voice in the back of my head was screaming to shoot but I hesitated.

The figure lifted his right hand and held up a gloved index finger. Black energy crackled around the gloved hand. It looked like reverse lightening, so dark it would blot out light. The energy faded from black to an angry red around the tip of his index finger. Suddenly, he twitched his finger and my pistol was shoved upwards like a bad Cagney and Lacey rerun. I literally thought it was going to fly out of my hands and over my head.

"If you wish to keep your weapon you will put it away", the man croaked. "I will not ask again." The figure still had his back to me. His voice, however, held a certainty that would have robbed anyone of their surety. Other than his hand he hadn't moved or even shifted. Still as a statue and cold as the grave.

What the hell was going on? Two trips into the land of hallucinations in one night. What were the chances that someone had slipped me something? LSD or 'shrooms maybe? This wasn't possible. This was something out of a movie.

"It is possible Mr. Magnus, and it is happening", the figure stated. "you would do well to stop thinking in circles and start accepting that this is your new reality. This is, what is, for you now".

"How are you reading my mind", I asked in an astonishment that was also tinged with a healthy dose of fear. I was way out of my league in this. Dude could read my mind. This definitely had to be LSD.

"Come here and sit down Mr. Magnus. I wish this to be a cordial discourse but my patience grows thin", the figure stated. That raspy voice now held a soul chilling menace and I knew without a doubt that if I did not obey I might never walk out of my apartment again.

I holstered my weapon and walked over to the scarred dinette table. I sat down in one of the creaking chairs so that I was facing the black shrouded figure. I noticed the figure had an athletic build under the trench coat but I got distracted by what was between us. The light I had seen coming from the kitchen was actually a burning flame hovering about eight inches off the table. It hovered burning cheerily with no fuel source and nothing to support it. The light felt diseased and cast twisted sickly shadows around the kitchen.

Seeing my uninvited guest's face for the first time shocked me. I had expected a desiccated corpse or talking skull with flaming eyes. Instead, a pale face sat framed by a black overcoat with a black long brimmed fedora perched on top of his head. Shaggy black hair fell gracefully from under the hat and glowed in the light. His face was stark with strong lines and a jaw as hard as stone. His nose had a fullness that would either give one beauty or mockery. I saw his eyes last. Maybe I didn't really want to see his eyes. They glittered a cold gray. Like they had their own snowfall inside them. Looking into the stranger's eyes made me feel like if anyone looked for too long they would freeze to death. The flaming skull might have been better.

"Do you like my little light Mr. Magnus", the man asked. "Witchfire is one of the simplest things to bring forth but very tricky", he continued while reaching up with his gloved hand to caress the air around the small light as if it were a pet.

"What do you want", I asked before blurting, "and who are you? How do you know my name, how did you get in here?" I was intent on knowing what the hell was going on. Who was this horror movie reject and why was he in my apartment? What did this have to do with what happened earlier tonight? I was starting to doubt my sanity less and less and just be angry. Anger was better than fear but fear would keep you alive. Anger just made you stupid.

"My name, Mr. Magnus, my name", the figure mused. "My name was lost long ago and would not matter to you either way". As the figure spoke I could feel an ominous foreboding as though knowing the figures name would just make the whole scene more dangerous. I'd known people before with no name. Killers and worse back when I worked for Dear Old Uncle Sam. If someone didn't want you to know their name it was generally a clue. "But for this conversation you may call me Marcus", the figure stated. On these words the darkness at the edge of the floating light seemed to buzz slightly, as though it was angry.

"Ok, Marcus, would you care to explain what is going on and how you knew my name", I asked, sounding way bolder than I felt. "I assume you have some reason for breaking in here and tormenting me with riddles." I was not going to be cowed by the freak show sitting across from me. I may die here but I was going to go out the way I had come in, screaming and covered in someone else's blood. It occurred to me that this may not be the best strategy for survival, but hey, the weirdness factor had triggered my smart ass button. Again, anger equals stupid.

"I knew your Grandmother Isabelle before she came to this country. I have known your family for a very long time", Marcus stated while looking me in the eyes. Looking into his eyes made me feel like Daffy Duck had just walked over my grave. "Your grandmother gifted you a cloth bag charm, a gris gris, as the hoodoo people call it, did she not", Marcus asked.

"How do you know about that", I demanded, while groping to make sure it was still in my left pocket. Finding it and pulling it out Marcus flinched back slightly. What the hell?

"Put that away Mr. Magnus lest I take it from you" Marcus hissed. The witchlight bobbed slightly causing the shadows to writhe around us. Was he afraid of it? Did his reaction have something to do with the gris gris bursting into flame tonight? Was Marcus a part of what had happened to me at that house? I held the gris gris in my left hand and eased it under the table. I wasn't going to put it up though. His reaction told me he didn't like it. Which meant that I might have some way to defend myself after all. I wasn't giving up a possible weapon if I didn't have too.

"Good, Mr. Magnus, at least you can listen", Marcus said. "So, listen now, for I will explain this only once", he said as if he was a storyteller and I was a willing audience. "I have known your family for many years. At times one or another of your bloodline has been challenged by Fate to fight against the denizens of the 'aradi alzili and others."

"Huh, what", I broke in, "throughout the years, fate, Godzilla what", I asked, showing my keen intellect. He was talking like somewhere I had a frame of reference for the conversation. "This sounds like some fairy tale my grandma told as a bedtime story", I said, clenching my hands in frustration. I understood the situation now. The dude was nuts and just needed a ride back to the hospital. His meds were off. At least it wasn't me.

"Shut up and listen", Marcus bellowed and slammed his fists onto the dinette table. The table must have been sturdier than I thought because his blow was hard enough to send it into the apartment below me. The witchlight flared to life and he had to grab it with both hands to make it settle. I thought it might leave scorch marks on the table. The darkness throughout the apartment coiled around itself. I could hear him take two or three rasping breaths in an attempt to calm himself. Dude needed to lay off the energy drinks and add anger management classes to his therapy routine. Maybe some yoga?

"I realize this is too much for your limited intellect, Mr Magnus, but you will hear me", Marcus stated. I could hear rage backing every word. He did not like being interrupted.

"Your people were gifted, or cursed, with a horrible responsibility before Sumer was a group of mud hovels. You have a responsibility to defend humans and others from the 'aradi alzili." Marcus kept talking like I was supposed to just magically understand.

"A rough translation of the words 'aradi alzili would be the shadow lands, though this is far from accurate. There are many realms outside of this one. At times your clan, and others, have been cursed to deal with, and sometimes war against, these other realms. In each realm, reality must have a balancer, a way to keep order", he continued, speaking as though to a recalcitrant child. As he continued on I shifted and checked the angles, looking for room to attack or run.

"Your family has been one of those balance points throughout the shadow lands and other realms besides. Your Grandmother Isabelle was a warrior such as this. She was a shrewd woman who could do many things". As Marcus spoke I could feel a pressure in my mind, a truth long untold being levied into my soul. "Isabelle passed down certain items to your mother, and through her to you, to help you survive should the curse come upon you. The gris gris is one, there was a necklace, a silver thing with a symbol of the people long hunted, for another" he explained.

"You mean that old Star of David necklace my mom wore", I asked a little stupidly.

"You still have it", Marcus demanded, leaning forward. His hands flexed on the table like he would claw through the cheap pressed wood. "Where is it", he asked with steel in his voice. Marcus had a serious want for the plain old necklace. His desire for the necklace left me with a strong need to keep it from him. Petty, I know, but call it a hunch. If he wanted it that badly I didn't think I should give it to him.

"I'm not really sure", I lied while thinking furiously. "I might have it in storage or I might have lost it in the divorce." Marcus did not need to know that the necklace was about thirty feet from him in my mom's old jewelry box. I hadn't kept much when my mom died but I had kept the necklace and the box. I didn't really know why, it just seemed important at the time.

"Might have lost it", he asked more to himself than to me. Marcus deflated somewhat and the witchlight dimmed. Looking at me suddenly with those frozen gray eyes he said, "Mr. Magnus I hope, for your sake, that this is not the case". The cold menace coming from him on this statement had me tensing my hand around the gris gris and preparing for a fight. He had a serious issue about this. Hell, the dude had more issues than Sports Illustrated period.

"Look, why does it matter", I asked. "You're sitting here telling me some bullshit about me being cursed or chosen like I'm a seventh son from an old blues song. It's bullshit. I'm just a guy, nothing special, nothing more. You need to get your meds checked pal, or maybe some electro shock therapy or something", I continued, raising my voice.

Marcus sat back and looked at me for a moment. His entire presence radiated anger and disdain. Yep, it was time to fight. I could feel the tension in the air solidify. We were going to rumble. I pushed my feet flat on the floor and prepared to lunge towards him. I may die here, but so would he.

Suddenly Marcus began to laugh. No, to howl, not just laugh. But it wasn't a jovial sound. Marcus sounded like a lunatic laughing over the corpses of those he had slaughtered. That laughter that only comes from moments of great horror and despair. From when something breaks inside of you and will never be whole again.

"I can see, Mr. Magnus, that you shall require more proof. This I will give you. Do you know the way to the intersection of Fourth and Trade St. in this township", he asked, suddenly cold as ice again. This dude had more ups and downs than a bipolar on a hobby horse.

"Where the Old Town Coffee Shop is", I asked. Of course, coffee shops were one of my major navigational landmarks. Coffee is life and I could tell you which barista worked by the smell of the brew as I walked in the door.

"I do believe there is a storefront such as you speak at this location", Marcus stated and appeared to shrug. It was hard to read his body language through all the unrelieved black. You'd think the guy taught potions somewhere. "Meet me there tonight at ten of the clock and I will show you proof, as my word is not good enough", he stated.

Turning away from Marcus I glanced at the clock on the oven. It was three in the morning now. As I looked back to explain that I had to work and couldn't meet him, he was gone. Just gone. The witchfire was all that remained, and it faded slowly, dwindling to the size of a match flame, then a spark, then nothing. Where the hell did he go? Thinking about that question, it may have been an answer as well.

Chapter Four

I'm standing on a highway at night. There's an overturned red minivan on the highway under a single streetlamp. The night is still. No breeze, no clouds, not even stars in the sky. Just the two lane blacktop stretching into the blank darkness in either direction. The smell of hot metal and spilling fuel fill the small bubble of the single street light. I can hear people screaming but their screams are faint and indistinct. They sound like they're screaming from far away.

I start to approach the minivan when I hear rustling in the darkness behind me. It leaves me with the vague impression that the night is grating on itself outside the bubble of light. I look away from the minivan and realize that what is behind me isn't the darkness of night. It is nothingness. This small bubble of light and asphalt is all of reality. There is nothing else.

From overhead I begin to hear a chittering noise. I've never heard anything like it. It sounds as though a hyena was cackling and a bat was chirping but all from the same voice box. Before I can look up to see what is above me I hear a small child speak.

"Excuse me, I think you dropped this", a small feminine voice says. All sound stops. The chittering from above, the slithering from out in the dark and the screaming from in the distance all cease at once. Turning to the voice I see a small child. Blond hair and bright blue eyes and a white sleeping gown stained with blood. She's holding her head on her bleeding neck with one hand.

Seeing her I cry out in shock and grief. I have to try and save her. I have to do something, I think in despair. I try to move towards her but I can't. I can't move my feet. Looking down I see blackness creeping over my boots and holding my feet in place. The black top of the road has encased my boots and is snaking its way up my legs in thin tendrils of writhing blackness. I'm helpless and cannot move to save the little girl. Again, the despair at my failure to save her crystallizes within me.

She moves towards me gliding on the blacktop. There's the illusion that she doesn't walk but floats towards me as her grubby blood stained nightgown drags across the ground. I want to tell her to stop. To cry out to her that she needs help but I can't seem to make a sound. The black tendrils continue to snake up my thighs as she moves closer. She raises her free hand towards me as she draws nearer. Dangling from her outstretched hand is my mother's necklace. As I see it the bright blue Star of David begins to glow and writhe on the small amulet. The star contorts around the little amulet like a living being.

Looking from the amulet to her face I watch in horror. Her beautiful five year old eyes bleach from that well remembered blue to a jaundiced yellow white. Her face begins to decompose in front of my eyes. I watch helpless as her left ear begins to separate. Her nose rots and falls to the blacktop with a soft wet sound. I scream as her lips draw up leaving her teeth exposed in a sickening grin as her gums blacken. A putrid smell of rot and decay assaults my senses as I struggle in the grip of the inky tendrils moving up my body. The beautiful child's body is rotting before my eyes, sickening my soul and leaving me retching in rage and pain. She thrusts the necklace towards me as maggots pour from her mouth and her head topples to the ground with a crash that shakes the entire bubble of our little reality.

I woke up screaming and sitting bolt upright in bed. I had two fistfulls of sheet where I had apparently shredded the bedding in my delirium. Covered in sweat and panting I stared sightless into the dark trying to understand the horror of the dream I had just experienced. My throat felt so raw I thought I had gargled with razor blades. I rolled off the bed and onto the floor retching and crying. With every scream and whimper I vomited onto the floor I could feel my heart break and my soul tear just that little bit more. This pain would never end. I felt spent and useless lying there.

Rolling onto my side I could see, through bleary tear damp eyes, that the closet door had a hole in it near where the top shelf would have been. Lying on the floor about a foot from my nose was my mother's jewelry box. It was a dark oaken thing about the size of a hardcover book. The box sat in the center of the floor perfectly upright with the lid open like it had been placed there. I knew it wasn't possible but it felt like the box had broken through the door and placed itself where I would see it as I lay on the floor. Could that be the crash I had heard which pulled me from the nightmare?

Crawling on my hands I peered inside the box. In the center was my mom's necklace. Where once had sat a normal tear drop shaped silver medallion with a simple Star of David was now a glowing piece of silver covered in shimmering white light. I hesitantly reached into the box, afraid of what might be happening and what I did not know. As my shaking fingers wrapped around the amulet my hand was covered in the silver white light. I brought the amulet out of the box so that I could see the Star in its center. But the Star wasn't the Star of David any longer. Instead, the symbol looked more like a drawing I had seen in an old magic book my grandmother had kept. It was still a hexagram but it now appeared to be more somehow. It had more depth and the lines were straight like they had been carved by a laser.

Focusing all of my shaken mind on the little amulet I watched as burning runes appeared around the outline of the hexagram forming a circle. The runes and the hexagram began to pulse with a red light akin to fire. I wrapped both hands around the amulet and thought hard about how I wished I understood what was happening. I felt the shape of the amulet change from that of a teardrop to a circle about the size of a silver dollar. Looking into my cupped hands I could see that the amulet had changed shape, which was impossible of course.

"What the fuck is going on", I bellowed in rage and confusion. I felt like everything I knew was slipping away from me.

"You don't have to yell deary, I'm dead not deaf", a voice said from beside me.

To my right sat my Grandmother Isabelle. My dead Grandmother Isabelle. She was sitting on the edge of my bed looking down on me with a smile as warm as sunshine and a mischievous twinkle in her hazel eyes. Wearing one of her signature blue farm dresses with a white apron she was a plump woman who could easily knead dough all day or strangle a chicken but was just as capable of soothing a little boys hurts with a kiss and a cuddle. Her auburn hair had long ago gone white and was cut shoulder length but still made her beautiful. She was the rose which time could not whither.

I scrambled back on all fours until my back hit the wall. I stared dully at my dead grandmother. "That's it", I said in a soft voice, "I've lost my fucking mind".

"Young man", Grandmother Isabelle barked while pointing a finger at me sternly, "I will nae brook such language from ye". I had forgotten how strong her brogue could get when she was angry. "I'll tan ye'r hide from here to tomorrow if'n ye use such language saving my presence". By the time I came along Grandma's Scottish accent had dwindled to the soft twang of the Appalachian Mountains but when she got fired up you could still hear the lilt of bonny Scotland in her voice.

"Yes Ma'am", I mumbled looking at her in amazement. Whatever this hallucination was, it looked and sounded just like I remembered her.

"Now that's settled why are ye staring at me with your mouth all open", Grandmother asked, "are ye daft lad?"

"Well Ma'am", I began stammering, "meaning no disrespect but you're dead".

Grandmother Isabelle began to laugh, tilting her head back and allowing the sound to fall like golden notes of mirth from her lips. "Aye deary, I'm dead, but that doesn'a mean I'm gone. I just ken things a wee bit different, no", she said while looking at me very directly.

"If you say so ma'am", I said, shaking my head and trying to accept what I was seeing. It suddenly occurred to me that I was very naked. Looking down and seeing my nudity I blushed to the roots of my hair. She was my grandmother and had changed some of my diapers, but that was different than being a grown man facing the shade of a woman I had loved and respected.

"Ah well lad", Grandma said as she noticed my predicament, "grab ye a pair of trousers and let's have us a chat, eh?"

I scrambled up from the wall and grabbed my jeans from the floor beside the bed. Struggling to get the jeans on I noticed her watching me with a disapproving expression. No one can do disapproving like a Scottish grandmother.

"Yes ma'am", I said in a questioning tone while trying not to sound slightly querulous. I knew she had a question and I suspected it would not be a happy one.

"Those marks on yer body, why did ye find them necessary", she asked. Her tone wasn't exactly judgmental. She was curious but I could also tell she disapproved.

"The scars or the tattoos ma'am", I asked stalling for time until I could get my mental sea legs.

"Yon scars I ken, your da and granda were bonny fighters", she said a bit wistfully, "but the tattoos, as ye call them, them I dinna understand". She looked me over carefully as though examining every inch of my inked flesh.

"Grandma, it's a long story and I'm confused enough. Would you please explain all this", I asked in exasperation while waving my hand about. The forgotten necklace and amulet had lain forgotten in my right hand until that moment.

"Ah, ye have it I see", she said with great satisfaction. "Put it on boy, it cannae help ye if ye dinnae wear the thing", she scolded. Thank goodness she wasn't buried with her wooden spoon or I'd probably have my knuckles wrapped. Or worse truth be told.

"What good is this going to do", I asked while holding the amulet at eye level. It still burned slightly with its own light in the darkness of my bedroom.

"Well, fer one it lets you see me now doesn't it", she asked, giving me a wink and a small nod. "That wee bauble is much older than it looks, ye ken", she continued. "If'n ye'll listen and pay a bit of attention yon wee piece will show ye the path and mightn't even keep ye from trouble I 'spect." Her accent was slipping from Scots to the Appalachian mountain talk more common at the end of her life.

"Ma'am", I asked, suddenly afraid. I hadn't seen her since I was a boy but I suddenly didn't want to lose her again.

"I could only visit fer a minute, ye understand", she said as she began to fade. I could just start to see the wall through her body. "Wear the bauble and the charm bag boy and beware Ma-", suddenly she was gone. The room was empty except for me and the smell of warm apples and cinnamon. Shaking my head I put the necklace around my neck and fixed the clasp. I felt a warm thrum through my body. I felt more complete with the amulet on. Like there had been a piece missing until now. I groaned in frustration and went to make coffee. Coffee cured everything, right?

Chapter Five

It was late afternoon when I finally left the apartment. I needed space to think. I had a bad case of mental whiplash from the events of the last twenty four hours and I needed perspective. I purposely cultivated the look of a knuckle dragging bad boy but I actually could read and write. I had advanced degrees in both Psychology and Criminal Justice. I wasn't the sharpest tack in the drawer but I had spent years thinking my way around problems and coming up with a workable answer on less than reliable data.

Coffee in hand and dressed warmly in a fresh pair of jeans, a hoodie and my favorite leather jacket I drove to the graveyard at Old Salem. Old Salem was originally a Moravian Settlement founded in 1766 by settlers from the Czech Republic. It was one of two towns which grew together over time to form modern day Winston Salem. The graveyard at Old Salem is a gothic masterpiece of statutes, crypts and mausoleums. I understand that sitting in a graveyard is not a particularly sane thing to do when troubled. Most folks spend their whole lives trying to stay out of graveyards, literally, and I liked to sit in them. But no one bothers you there and it's a wonderfully quiet place to sit and think. Quiet as the grave really.

I sat on the eastern wall watching the sun set in the west over Highway 52. The past twenty four had been a confusing riot of experiences I hadn't been able to process yet. Sipping my coffee I huddled tighter into my leather jacket as the wind ripped over the cobblestone paths and through the grave stones. I couldn't stop wondering what it all could mean. I was beginning to accept that I wasn't completely bat shit crazy. I mean, I'd always been crazy, anyone who runs towards fire while everyone else runs away is seriously messed up in the head. But I refused to fail to adapt to new circumstances. Flexibility of thought is more important to survival than holding on to preconceived notions. Going on that assumption I had to try to see a logical pattern to the events. Or just a pattern since I wasn't sure logic applied to ghosts of dead relatives and ghouls who wanted to devour me. I mean I know I look delicious but that was the most extreme reaction I'd ever had from a man or a woman.

In the past day I had seen an old woman transform into a putrid breasted beast hungry for flesh. I'd watched a doll walk on its own and thank me. I'd had a bizarre visit from the mummy's goth reject cousin who could juggle fire and my deceased grandma had sat on the edge of my bed and seen me naked. And the dreams, the dreams had taken a sickening turn. It was definitely a red letter day for Cy. Whiskey Tango Foxtrot, for real.

As the sun gave one more glorious burst of pink and purple on the horizon before sinking to the depths of long lost night I decided to head back to my car. In my time sitting on the ancient stone wall I had decided that I had to meet Marcus. I had to know more. Not just because I wanted to understand but because I felt that the lack of intel might very well get me killed. Admitting I had a problem was the first step really. Not getting my cock blown off while trying to figure it out was the second.

It was dusk but not fully dark as I walked across the parking lot to my car. The wind was as cruel as a pimp's heart and cut through me like a straight razor. Leaves and dust blew in streamers across the barren landscape. Unlocking the doors with the remote I got in and settled for a moment. That last shiver from the icy wind racked my spine as leaves blew across the windshield. In the silence of the car I felt that something wasn't right. I don't know what it was. Maybe it was a slight shift in the weight of the car or a subtle smell but I knew something wasn't right. I was not alone in this car.

Fear shot through me as I felt someone behind my seat. My breath choked and my heart jack hammered as my body remembered what to do from years of training. There was no conscious thought. My monkey brain was trying to process as my lizard brain took charge and decided to handle the threat. The monkey brain could catch up later.

Pulling a long thin blade from the inner lining of my jacket I reversed my grip so the blade extended from the bottom of my fist and twisted to stab into the back seat area of the car. "Slow is smooth and smooth is fast", my old instructors had taught me and I had practiced this until the entire motion was as smooth as silk gliding along the body of a lover. As the blade arched over the back seat a black blur reached out and caught my arm at the wrist. My arm stopped dead. There was no give in the grip of whatever had me. My pulse was pounding in my throat.

"Mr. Magnus I do believe you do not like me", a voice said from the backseat. Turning I could see the pale face of Marcus staring at me. All I could see was the faint outline of his body and his stark white face as the black of his clothes blended with the thick darkness of the back seat. The macabre scene of the angular face floating in the dark was surreal. He continued to hold my arm so firmly that I wasn't sure if I would be able to get it back.

"Why, because I'm always drawing weapons when I see you", I snarled back at him. My fear had turned to anger again and I was really considering pushing the destruct button. One of us would make it and one of us wouldn't. "Why in the hell are you sitting in the back seat of my car in the dark and where the hell did you come from", I demanded hotly. My muscles were corded with tension and I was shaking from the adrenaline going through my body.

"I did not think you would come to meet me tonight so I decided to meet you", he was utterly and icily calm. "What was it Ms. Dickenson said? 'Because I could not stop for death so he kindly stopped for me'? Or some such?", he quoted the line like it was a happy thought and not creepy as hell.

"'The carriage held but just ourselves, and immortality'", I quoted back at him.

"Mr. Magnus I did not know you were a man of letters", Marcus said. He seemed genuinely surprised. Glad my knowledge of poetry impressed him since trying to stab him sure didn't. He still sat, holding my arm in a vice-like grip.

"'Because I Could Not Stop For Death' is one of Emily Dickenson's most taught poems in high school", I said flippantly. Damned if he was going to see just how wigged out I was by the conversation.

"Ah", he said. "I learn new things about you every day Mr. Magnus", he said with a grin. It wasn't a pleasant grin. It was too sinister for that. Like he was imagining me without my skin and happy about it.

"Let us be off, I would hate for you to miss our appointment", Marcus said.

"Did you consider that you might miss the appointment if I killed you", I asked very quietly.

"Mr. Magnus, missing an appointment with death is a thing to be celebrated", he said with a kind of wistful relish. He suddenly released my arm. It throbbed like from the sudden return of blood flow.

"Do you like graveyards Mr. Magnus", he asked in a quiet almost wistful tone. He turned his head to look out the window towards the night shrouded graveyard.

I was busy trying to massage the blood back into my arm and hand. Sliding the blade back into the hidden sheath in the lining of my jacket I asked, "you mean when people are not creeping around in my back seat".

Marcus slowly turned his head back to me. Watching him turn his head reminded me of some big predator slowly sizing up a meal. As his frosty gray eyes locked with mine I knew I was in danger and I absolutely did not care. I would not be stalked or bullied and that was the hill I was prepared to die on. I would not flinch back or bow down and I refused to be afraid of anyone. I looked Marcus square in the eyes and would not look away. As we stared into each others eyes in a supreme moment of machismo I felt my gris gris begin to burn in my thigh pocket. My palms began to itch and my breathing picked up. The fight was coming, it was just a question of who made the first move.

"Did you know my wife and daughter are buried there", Marcus asked softly.

"Buried where", I asked. The sudden segue was too fast for me.

"The graveyard you were just in, of course", he said in a disturbingly quiet voice. He was still staring at me with way too much intensity but the overall feel of the conversation had turned eerie. "After they were buried I decided to travel the world, but I always return Mr. Magnus", he explained, "yes, I always return". I was wishing he'd stop explaining. The more he talked the more wigged out I got. Every word conjured feelings of foreboding and doom. Dude was a serious buzz kill. He was the definition of a fun sponge.

"Why do you come back", I asked. I didn't want to know. But the part of me that was a cop, would always be a cop, could never let something like that go. Even when the irrational part of my brain was slamming the bars of its cage and screaming in warning.

"Their deaths, Mr. Magnus, started me on my quest. It was a polarizing moment for me. That moment set me on my path. I feel that it is only proper to return and remember them, no matter how harsh such remembrances are", he said all this as though he was the only person in the whole world.

"That's a rough thing and I'm very sorry that happened", I said while trying to be empathetic. I didn't like the guy but I could still be a reasonably good human being. Maybe even the crypt keeper could have feelings, right?

A moment of silence happened. The air was heavy with tension and was beginning to smell stale in the small car. The wind was still blowing ferociously outside. Full dark had settled in around us. We could have been the only two people left on Earth. There was an alarming thought.

"Sorry", Marcus whispered. He lunged forward, "Sorry", he bellowed. Spit was flying from his mouth as he roared at me. His eyes seemed to glow with a red light. "Sorry is for weaklings, it is for the dead", he screamed inches from my face. "I watched my wife and child die, Mr. Magnus, for nothing", he yelled. Marcus seemed to pulse with rage and hate. "I cleaned their bodies and sewed their burial shrouds", he continued. "And once they were in the frozen earth I sought to become so much more than a simple minister bound to a lost religion". Marcus had gone from distant, to enraged and down to an icy hissing calm in the space of a minute. There really was a heavy sense of madness to Marcus. Not the current mental health driven understanding of mental illness but the old school fire and brimstone something from beyond madness that could lead someone to destroy towns and murder innocents while listening to a dark symphony of voices in one's own mind.

I sat there waiting for a moment. I was unsure of what would happen next. I had no problem fighting Marcus. Dude tripped my shoot now and ask questions later switch. But he was also the only one willing to explain anything right now. I couldn't trust him, but I could go along for the ride until I figured out who was good and what was evil.

"Drive, Mr. Magnus, drive us to where we need to be", Marcus said after several moments.

Not knowing what else to do I cranked the car, put it into drive and turned back to ask Marcus, "Hey, do you like coffee?"

Chapter Six

It took about ten minutes of driving to reach the Old Town Coffee Shop at Fourth and Trade St. Downtown Winston Salem was an interesting mixture of buildings from back when big tobacco owned everything to modern high rises with the occasional historic era house or building cozied up in a nook somewhere as though hiding the history of the city in the dark shadows of modernization. The coffee shop was in what had once been an office building from the forties or fifties. The old courthouse was about a block down Fourth St and the original lynching grounds were about three miles down Liberty St. from where I was now. Ah, history. Now the whole area was home to some of the best coffee and pimento cheese sandwiches in the area. It was good to see someone willing to keep the old building alive.

I parked the car and we exited the vehicle. I couldn't wait to head in and get a cup of something to warm me. The cold was intense. Before entering the cheery warmth I stopped for a moment and just took in the ambiance of the area at night. There was always a different energy to any town's downtown district after dark. It always had the feeling that the buildings and back alleys were only ever truly alive after dark. Maybe the human stain forced the energy of the area to be still until late at night when it could be itself.

This block of Fourth Street was mainly turn of the century architecture that still had bomb shelter placards in place outside the doors. Two and three story buildings that gave off an air of age and exhaustion like long silent sentinels eroded by the passage of humanity. We humans tend to do that, erode the beauty of all which surrounds us. There was one building that had always stood out to me though. It was a two story storefront covered in old gray slate. It had once been Harper's Electric and probably thirty other things over the years. Large glass windows lined the front so that shoppers could see the wares of the day. It still had the granite slab steps leading to the front door that were so prevalent in that era. But what really made it stand out were the two large lion statues that stood to either side of the entrance. They were carved with a quiet dignity that still left you feeling as though they could come alive at any moment.

Marcus watched me watching the statues before asking, "Do you know what animus and anima are, Mr. Magnus?" His voice seemed to reverberate slightly among the darkened recesses of the old buildings. There was a sibilant reverb from his voice to the shadows and back that left me with the fleeting thought that the two might be connected.

"Animus is life right", I asked. I wanted to be careful about how much I admitted I knew about anything. I wanted Marcus to continue thinking I was some illiterate knuckle dragger. I had slipped up in the car and needed to fix his impression of me. Playing the dumb cop had let me learn many things in life and was great around suspects.

"You surprise me Mr. Magnus", Marcus said.

"I do have a library card", I replied, getting a little annoyed. Okay I was apparently succeeding at appearing stupid but his arrogance was starting to piss me off.

"Yes, of course", Marcus sneered. "And did you learn in your library that inanimate objects made in the form of something living are called anima", he asked.

"You mean like statues or dolls", I asked, trying to follow. Did he know about the doll at the putrid breast demon's house?

"Yes, very astute, Mr. Magnus", Marcus stated patronizingly. "Dolls, statues, carvings and even old paintings at times can be what we term anima. Anima are vessels which have the ability to be possessed by beings from different realms", he continued. He spoke in a very patronizing manner as though I had been dropped on my head as a child.

"And animus is the entity possessing such an anima", I asked. My pride was getting the better of me. I had to demonstrate that I could comprehend the conversation for my own self respect.

"Very good Mr. Magnus, this may not be as difficult as I thought", he said and almost lightened up for a moment. Almost.

"Be careful Marcus, you spoke to me like a real person" I said with a soft chuckle.

Marcus stared at me for a moment before saying, "Oh you are a person, Mr. Magnus". Something in the way he said that made me wonder if he thought he wasn't and that humans were a lesser species.

Marcus looked at me for a moment longer before quietly saying, "look at the statues Mr. Magnus". His voice was utterly calm. He stood motionless as though he could stand there blending into the shadows for a century and never move.

I turned from Marcus to look back at the old statues. The lions were carved so that their bodies faced the street but their heads were turned towards each other. Like they were expected to examine each person who entered the building. Strangely they were now both staring at me. The one on my right tilted his head to the side quizzically as though trying to understand what it was seeing. They were stone and yet now I perceived an intelligence and aliveness they had not had a moment before. The one on the left opened its mouth wide in a silent roar before shaking itself and resuming its pose on the pedestal, endlessly waiting.

My quest for coffee and answers momentarily forgotten, I moved towards the statues. I couldn't believe what I was seeing. In that one moment I forgot the cold, the wind, and the ghoulish figure of Marcus. It was almost as though I could hear the animus inside the statue. It was a whisper just on the outside of hearing. I was certain if I held still and slowed my breathing I would just be able to hear what it was saying. I couldn't seem to concentrate on anything else. They were mesmerizing.

A loud blaring horn startled me from my trance. I was in the middle of Fourth Street. Blinding lights were to my left and the horn was about to make my ears bleed. I rolled across the far lane and tumbled to the sidewalk. I lay there panting as realization dawned on me that I had wandered directly into traffic. A very large truck had almost turned me into street meat. I was just almost killed staring at the impossible site of the animated statues. The sidewalk was cold under me but the sweat running down my spine was even colder. Damnit, what was wrong with me?

"Come along Mr. Magnus, this is no time to lay around", Marcus said as he floated past me. He glided past the statues and up the steps, disappearing into the dark of the store.

I laid there for a minute guppy gulping air and trying to decide whether I wanted to follow him or leave his ass here. I could be having a much better night with safer company if I'd just walk back up the street and into the coffee shop. But since stubborn is my main personality trait I got up, dusted myself off and approached the lions. They looked at me and scented the air like they really had lungs, but they did not interfere with me entering. As I topped the steps and looked back, both had become statues again. Not an ounce of life about them.

Walking through the antique glass doors of the building I could feel the difference in the air. It smelled musty like one would expect from somewhere long disused. But it was more than that. There was a feeling of oppression that hit me as soon as I walked in. That doomed feeling like there should have been a sign over the door that read "abandon all hope all ye who enter here". I found that I had automatically taken my gris gris from my pants pocket. Pulling my trusty flashlight out I followed Marcus's dusky shadow as he moved wraithlike towards the rear of the building. I could see where the building had once been a very fancy place. Once this had been a place people had probably been proud to work in. Now it was just empty and abandoned, lonely in its lost use. Old crown mold still hung on the walls in places. Handcrafted chair molding clung in spots around the open room. Marcus didn't seem to make noise as he walked through the open bay of the building. Every surface was covered in dust from being empty for so long. The old wooden floorboards creaked and groaned as I followed him, but he made no sound. Maybe I needed to go on a diet?

Marcus stopped near the back wall and turned to face me. Though honestly the only way I could tell he was facing me was the pallor of his skin floating in the dark. The inky blackness emphasized the paleness of his skin. He held one gloved finger to his lips then motioned towards a stairwell leading to a sub level of the building. The stairwell had been invisible in the gloom until that moment. The great ghoul wanted me to head down into the basement of an abandoned building at night. This was a really stupid move I thought to myself and looked around the room one more time. But how else was I going to figure this out? Wanting answers more than sanity I stepped around Marcus and started down the steps. I knew this was going to be bad. I just knew it.

Chapter Seven

The thick wooden steps were dark and bowed beneath my weight. They felt rotten under me. The stairwell itself was a stygian darkness. Without my flashlight I could've touched my own eyeball and I would have never seen my finger. I eased down the stairs one step at a time. Cobwebs kept brushing my face and neck like that old Indiana Jones flick from the eighties. I might be trying to walk quietly but if a spider suddenly fell down my shirt I was going to lose it. I didn't have a flamethrower with me but I was sure I'd figure out something more destructive than foul language. I was trying to move silently but the old wood and tight quarters of the stairwell caused groaning echoes to sound through the claustrophobic stairwell and echo back up from the basement.

I was almost to the foot of the stairs when a figure appeared out of the gloom. It was a tall man holding a weak lantern at shoulder level and glaring up at me. He was dressed in old fashioned breaches and a worn white and blue striped shirt with an even more worn apron covering the front of his body. As I stepped closer I could see antique wire rim glasses perched on his stentorian nose. He looked like an angry nineteenth century shopkeeper. With emphasis on the angry. He seemed to visibly vibrate with a silent rage. Why did everyone Marcus bring me to need anger management classes? Didn't he have happy friends?

"So, what am I supposed to do down here", I asked the angry man.

He turned without a word and moved off into the basement. I hurried to follow him, almost breaking my neck rushing down the last two steps. He had turned and walked away like I wasn't really there. As though he saw and comprehended my presence on one level but I didn't phase into his world on another. He was slowly striding deeper into the room. The only two lights were coming from the weak flame of the lantern and my small flashlight. I couldn't see anything outside of the cone of light from the lantern. As the silent angry man walked deeper into the darkness I noticed a white circle carved into the floor. The man stopped in the center of the circle and turned smartly to face me. Almost parade ground perfect.

The man glared at me for a moment more and then dropped the lantern to the floor. It cracked at his feet and the flame spilled from the lantern. The flame changed color from a normal orange and yellow to the sick green of pestilence and decay. It began twisting and undulating around the man's feet before sliding sinuously along the floor to the carved circle. The flame moved with an intelligence all its own. I had seen this before, or something similar. What Marcus had called witchfire. As the witchfire completed the circle its light illuminated the basement. The walls were moving shadows of madness. Writhing faces morphed in and through the walls. Faces of men, women and children wore a range of expressions. Anger, sadness, horror, pain, and even laughter. The faces expressed thousands of moments in millions of lives all trapped within the shadow walls of this room. They flexed in and out of the walls like sentient Rorshachs trapped within the stone. Their bodies mangled or emaciated beyond belief. The witchfire grew taller as it filled the circle, becoming a foot high wall of sickly green fire. The contrast of the green from the fire and the constantly dancing shapes in the walls made me want to wretch. It was hell's own psychedelic wall art.

I was quickly growing addled. I couldn't focus enough to even draw a weapon. And even if I could, which threat was imminent? I was in a basement where everything was death. I fell to my knees as the horrific dance of shadow and light continued to grow in intensity. On my knees on the stone floor I felt a burst of rage. I was not going to die like this! White hot fury coursed through me. This was not how I was going to end my existence! I screamed wordlessly into the dark! And suddenly I knew what to do. It was there in my mind. I couldn't run down the street yelling "eureka", but I could do other things. Worse things. I guess if you scream loudly enough the universe answers.

I drew my folding combat knife from my front right pocket and my gris gris from my left. I twisted the wrist of my right hand and six inches of well made steel spilled out of the handle. Focusing my anger and my sheer stubborn will to live through my hands and into the blade I stood to face the flame wreathed man. My hands were encased in blue energy. It was time to ruin his day. Believing that the best way to lose a fight is to talk about it, I started forward into the flames intending to gut the bastard.

A crash resounded behind me and I was swallowed by a rolling cloud of dust and asbestos. I spun looking for yet another threat. The upper floor had crashed down into the basement sending loose boards and rubble cascading over the stone floor. The dust and debris mixed with the witchfire creating an odd dance of clouds and green light. Standing on top of the rubble was a woman. It was hard to make out her features but light was streaming down from the hole in the floor casting her in a halo effect.

The woman stood maybe five foot seven with an athletically thick build. Think of a powerlifter who didn't lose her curves by adding muscle. A woman who could never be mistaken for anything else even if she was deadlifting you. Dark shoulder length hair glistened in the streaming light from above. She wore jeans and a leather vest and carried a long knife in her right hand. Her left hand was balled into a fist and burned with a silver light. She was beautiful violence in a place of horror. My hormones kicked over for just a second. Bad Cy, down boy! She was the woman of my dreams. Or possibly just my fantasies.

"Move, dumbass", she yelled at me as she charged forward. I dove out of her way and scrambled along the floor to get up and back into a fighting stance. She charged towards the witchfire yelling a primal battle cry at the beast which now filled the circle. What had been the angry man had morphed or mutated into a half rotted corpse. Its eyes and nose had rotted away and were empty black holes in a cadaverous face. The monster's hands were now boney claws encased in rotten flesh. It's skin was stretched taught along the bones of it's body like ancient leather worn thin. The bones of it's shoulders had grown out to spikes and it's rib cage had grown wisps of bone that poked through the skin. It's narrow hips and long boney legs were also covered in the tendrils of bone poking through like streamers. It reached for the screaming woman as she closed with it and rotting ichor streamed from it's mouth and down it's chin. In for a penny in for a pound I thought as I moved forward towards the two figures. She might be the epitome of sex and lust ready to brawl, but whoever she was, she would need help with this thing. An entire platoon of Marines would need help with this thing!

The woman slashed at the beast's head and missed as it ducked under her swing. It moved with a surprising grace considering it was a rotting corpse. The thing struck her squarely in the stomach. She flew backwards into the dark and the nimbus of silver light disappeared with her.

As I flanked the rotted thing, blue fire exploded around my hands. I drove my combat knife into its neck. The metal entering the rotted flesh made a wet squishing sound and I drew the blade out and through the back of the monster's neck. Pus and gore exploded from the half severed head of the putrid beast as it stumbled back and forth.

"You cannot stop us", it screamed in a high pitched voice. The beast was on the ropes but it wasn't dead yet. "The King is coming and he will destroy you all!" I grabbed the thing's shoulder and shoved it to the ground before stomping its skull into rancid black jelly. Finally, the thing stopped moving and the witchfire began to dim and shrink. What king was coming? What the hell was with the evil monologue?

Panting I looked around the basement trying to find the mysterious goddess who had intervened in the horror show. I was really going to have to start doing more cardio. She stood slowly from the debris, her hand once again glowing with the silver light. She shook her head causing her thick dark hair to swirl around her. The witchfire had faded to nothing and the only source of light was from the hole she had broken in the floor above us. She stood at the edge of the ring of light, half visible in the gloom. Covered in dust and fresh from battle she was one of the most beautiful women I had ever seen. She turned her head to look at me and I could see that her eyes glowed violet.

"Why are you here", she asked. Her voice had an accent, something I couldn't place. European, or maybe vaguely Russian? She was turning to face me more squarely and I felt a quick thrill of danger. I could tell she was sizing me up, trying to decide if I was friend or foe.

"Listen", I said, "it's not that I'm not grateful for your help, but who the hell are you lady?"

"Did you think you could raise this monster and have it do your bidding", she asked with a great deal of menace in her voice. Her hand was flexing around her knife and the silver nimbus was getting stronger. If I didn't explain quickly I was going to tote one hell of an ass whooping. I liked it rough, but not like this.

"What are you talking about", I demanded, "I killed that... whatever it was after it knocked you flying".

"Yes I suppose you did", she said, "for that I am grateful. I am known as Lila". She made no attempt to offer to shake my hand but I could tell she was toning down her intent to maim and murder. The violet light in her eyes was beginning to dim somewhat.

"My name is Cy and I'm glad you came when you did", I said while trying to focus on the conversation and not the raw beauty of the woman in front of me. I smiled at her and saw one corner of her mouth raise slightly.

"Why were you here with that zala" she asked. I could tell she was intent on getting an answer.

"An angry crypt keeper named Marcus led me here", I said as I realized that Marcus was nowhere to be seen. "What's a zala", I asked.

"A zala is a shade from one of the realms of the Shadow Realms", Lila stated somewhat pedantically. I remembered the reference from my first conversation with Marcus. "You seem as though you are a good man, you should stay away from that ghoul Marcus", she stated.

"I'm starting to get that feeling", I said with some frustration. I still didn't understand what was going on but I trusted her read on Marcus. The guy definitely creeped me out and I was beginning to see that he was a bigger problem than a help.

"Take this", Lila said and drew a large silver knife from a sheath on her thigh. She pitched it to me underhand and I caught it by the hilt as it flew slowly towards me. The handle was ribbed like ram horn and the blade had weird sigils carved along one side of its spine. "If you have dealings with Marcus you will surely need it", she said as she turned to walk into the darkness.

"Lila, wait, what do you mean", I asked, but somehow I knew that she was already gone. Disappeared into the shadows and whatever strange world she had come from. I hefted the blade and found it was balanced perfectly. I turned and stumbled back towards the stairs leading out of the basement. The place was empty now. Nothing left but the dying echoes of time. I made it safely back to my car. Marcus had vanished back to whatever freakish hell he had a weekend pass from and I was alone in the frozen night. I sat waiting for the car to warm up so I could begin to thaw out. The temperature was cold but the howling wind made the night feel like a wasteland of desolation and darkness as it clawed along my body and stole my warmth. The more of these encounters I had the less I could hope that my life would ever return to normal. But, then again, who the hell wanted to be normal anyway?

Chapter Eight

I was sleeping peacefully for the first time in months. I had wrapped myself into a naked tattooed burrito of warmth and was swaddled happily in my blankets. There was very little heat in the apartment on a good day and in the frozen hours of the night it was about five degrees warmer than a meat locker. I had enough blankets on my bed to drown in and I was snuggled deep under all of them.

I was roused by a loud banging echoing through the apartment. I tried to ignore it, I really did. I rolled over pulling my pillow over my head and trying to drown out the sound. I absolutely did not want to leave my cocoon of warmth. The knocking sounded again. It wasn't a normal person's knocking. Rather, this was a full on door frame rattling police knock. The kind that said they knew you were in there and you better already be on the ground showing your hands.

The knocking sounded a third time and I threw my pillow across the room angrily. Not really a temper tantrum, but not far from it either. Stomping down the hall, naked except for the small quilt drawn around my massive frame I walked to the door considering gruesome murder for the person outside. This was a great example of why I disliked basic human interaction at times. It was cold enough in the little apartment that I was sure my testicles wouldn't descend again until July and I had been jolted out of the first real sleep I'd had in months. Funny how a little combat let me sleep like a baby. I huddled further under the quilt and leaned against the wall beside the door.

"What do you want", I yelled through the door. It wasn't the most polite of greetings but I wasn't in a sociable mood.

"Cy, it's Clara", I heard through the door. "I brought coffee," Her voice lilted upward on the last word.

I couldn't yell at Clara. Her heart was always in the right place. She was a damned good friend and just an overall good person. Sometimes I thought I could see the goodness shining from her eyes. She might be a little innocent overall and very vanilla in her lifestyle, but there wasn't anything wrong with that. She was doing better than I was in the overall game of life. Besides, she had brought coffee. It was really hard to yell at someone when they bore such a holy substance.

"Coffee from where", I asked through the door. It was a petty question but I wanted to know if the coffee was good enough to wake up this early.

"It's Mama Diaz's special blend; but if you don't want it", her voice trailed off like she was walking away. I ripped at the lock and tore the door open to find her holding two cups of coffee and laughing softly at me. Her eyes twinkled with mirth at how fast I jerked the door open. That is, right up until the wind screamed down the hallway and we both realized that I was completely naked under the flapping quilt. I saw her look down, see more than she had ever seen of me and blush furiously. But she didn't look back up.

"Hey, eyes up here", I said, "what do you think I am a piece of meat"? In all honesty I was trying to distract her from the sight of me naked. I wasn't embarrassed per se but it was really cold out here. Didn't want to give the lady the wrong impression. I did tuck the quilt more firmly around my waist. You know, for her modesty and all.

"Should I take the coffee and leave", Clara asked, blushing furiously. She sounded almost normal but there was a hint of breathiness to her words. I stood back out of the way and motioned for her to enter. I felt bad that I had flashed her. I had suspected that she had a crush for a long time but I had never been sure. And she had been respectful of the fact that I was married and would never cross that line or put me in that kind of situation. But now, the heat in her eyes coupled with the raw hunger that had flashed across her face had been almost alarming.

Clara walked past me staring carefully down the hall as she passed me. She handed me my coffee then stopped. Looking back at me she said, "you smell horrible".

I raised my arm and sniffed. "Ugh yeah that's really bad" I said. I realized that I had gotten some of the zala's blood or puss on me without realizing it. I didn't just stink, I was funky, and not in the fun funkadelic kind of way. It was a smell that would gag a garbage man in August.

"Why don't I take your coffee to the kitchen and you go shower", Clara asked. She reached for the steaming cup of heaven.

"I'll shower but the coffee goes with me", I said, drawing the coffee back and looking at her menacingly. She laughed again and shook her head as she went to the kitchen and I headed to the shower. I threw the blanket near the clothes hamper to be washed eventually. Turning the shower on as hot as I could stand it I hopped in and started to thaw.

While boiling myself under the hot water I heard the bathroom door creak open. I heard Clara enter the bathroom and I peaked out from behind the curtain to see her lounging against the messy counter of the sink sipping her coffee.

"Clara, what are you doing", I asked. I was really glad she was still clothed but I was a little uncomfortable with the way this was playing out. I didn't think she would actually undress and join me but, until a minute ago, I didn't think she would ever look at me as a woman looks at a man.

"I'm just trying to figure out what's going on with you, Cy", she said. The words felt wistful and a little longing. Like a kid wondering why their best friend had run away.

"What do you mean", I asked while letting the soap suds trail down my body. I was scrubbing every inch of myself trying to find the patch of stench left on my flesh.

"I'm worried about you", she said. "You've cut yourself off", she continued, "we almost never talk, you're working this asinine job, and then you get jumped but can't tell me anything about what happened"? Her voice was growing hot with frustration and hurt as she continued, "you're like Conan the Barbarian and you remember details about perps like you were a computer".

"So, what's your point", I asked while sputtering water.

"Damn it Cy", she said, "I know you're lying and I know that you're avoiding me and I want to know why".

"Okay", I said, sighing. "Meet me in the living room and I'll tell you what I can". I knew she wouldn't believe me but I wasn't going to lie to someone I cared about.

"Really", Clara squeaked in astonishment. I could tell she was confused by my sudden capitulation.

"Unless you intend to watch me get out of this shower wet and soapy", I taunted.

"Well, Maybe", she started to say. I grabbed the edge of the shower curtain and started to yank it open.

"Okay, okay", Clara said quickly and fled the bathroom as I finished yanking open the shower curtain, standing nude and wet. I guess her nerves gave out. I toweled off and dressed in gray sweatpants and a comfortable faded cotton shirt with the SWAT emblem printed on it.

Walking into the living room I found Clara sitting on my second hand couch, coffee forgotten on the table, reading through one of my notebooks. She seemed intent on what she was reading. It was such an odd sight to see this person who exuded so much energy sit so still and quiet. I just stood in the doorway and watched her read. I very rarely let anyone read my work and published what few I did under a pen name. Her soft brown skin and the texture of her hair created a portrait in time of a young beautiful woman lost in her thoughts.

Clara saw me standing in the doorway and smiled at me. "I've never gotten over the fact that you write poetry", she said.

"What, I can't have depth", I asked while walking to the old stereo and starting some music. The gentle strains of old blues music eased from the speakers.

"It's not that you can't have depth, it's just that you try so hard to get people to think that you're this rough and tumble guy and you're really not", she replied.

"Cy can read, he he", I said in a fake caveman voice and then had to duck as Clara threw an ink pen at me.

"Seriously, Cy, you're such a talented guy", she said. "I still remember the first thing you told me when I was a rookie".

"Good doesn't triumph over evil but good people must always stand against evil", we quoted together.

"Words to live by", I said to Clara.

"And that's another thing that's worrying me, do you still live by anything", she asked.

"What do you want from me Clara", I asked her.

"I want to know what's going on with you and I want to know that you're okay", she said.

"I'm okay, I promise", I told her, "there's just a lot going on and I'm having to work through everything".

"Like what", she asked simply. Weak sunlight was streaming in through a crack in the curtains illuminating her face. Mr. Johnson strummed in the background. I could see the set to her jaw and the slight squint of her eyes and knew I wasn't going to be able to keep her out of it. When she set her mind to something she was stubborn.

"Well, the other night no one tried to rob me", I said. Screw it, let's see if she dealt with it better than I did. It was better to have her in cop mode than for me to see her as a woman. The uniform made us all the same. Or it should anyway.

"I knew it", she crowed and bounced up and down on the couch.

"I was attacked by a putrefied pus monster called a zala from the shadow lands and I killed it with a flaming mop handle", I said in a rush. Rubber room here I come!

"Okay Cy, now tell me the truth", she said, laughing.

"I'm serious", I said. "Apparently the paranormal is a real thing and I have been chosen, or whatever, to deal with it."

"Cy, what the hell are you talking about", she demanded. Clara was nine shades of pissed. Guess she didn't believe me. Which was reasonable since I wasn't sure I believed me either.

I had an idea. I didn't think it would work but I would try it. She couldn't think I was any crazier. "Do you trust me Clara", I asked?

"I'm starting to wonder", she said.

I walked over to my leather jacket which I had slung across the worn recliner. Reaching into the pocket I pulled out the blade Lila had given me last night. Turning to face Clara I held the blade low by my side. I could see her tense. We might be friends, but we were still cops. Caution keeps you alive. I focused my thoughts into the blade and willed the weird blue light to surround the blade as it had around my combat knife the night before. Blue flames burst from my hand and surrounded the knife. Clara yelped and half crawled half dove over the back of the couch. She didn't have cover but she did have concealment. She peered back over the top of the couch and I could tell she had her duty weapon out. I didn't think she would really shoot me but I didn't want to startle the woman with the gun.

"What the hell", Clara demanded.

"You weren't going to believe me unless you saw for yourself" I told her. "I don't believe it myself, to be honest, but last night I was attacked by an angry spirit that's apparently called a zala. The other night it was something else, I don't know what it was. Just that it was ugly and going to kill me. I would tell you more, hon, but I don't even know what's going on yet."

She stared at me taking deep breaths. She slowly stood from behind the couch as a new blues song began to play. She hadn't holstered up yet so I decided to remain very still. Clara walked towards me slowly, her gun forgotten in her hand, mesmerized by the blue flames surrounding my hand and the knife. She reached out carefully and waved her hand through the flames.

"It's not hot", she said softly.

"So far the flames only seem to bother the things trying to kill me", I told her. I had been half afraid the flames would burn her. I guess maybe they only hurt the monsters? I didn't have enough data for a hypothesis yet.

"So you're like some weird monster hunter off of TV", she asked. "Did you buy an old car too?" She was obviously yanking my chain. But she seemed to believe me so I could handle it.

"Clara I don't know what I am except the same old Cy", I told her. "I don't know what any of this means or what it looks like. I haven't even had time to process any of this."

"Ok, so explain what you do know", she said. She withdrew and sat back down on the couch. I put the blade down on the living room table and started talking. I told her everything. Marcus, Lila, the dreams and even the Raggedy Anne doll. She took it all in and I could tell she'd be able to quote it back to me later or testify to it in court if necessary. Somehow I didn't think a court would have jurisdiction over this.

Clara sat in silence when I finished. I could tell she was processing everything I had said. It was a lot to sort through. Or, at least, it was for me. Finally, I couldn't live with the silence any longer and asked, "do you believe me?"

"It's hard to believe Cy", she said while sighing, "but yes I do believe you. What's your next move", she asked.

"Well, I'm going to try and track down Lila and see what she can tell me", I explained. "Maybe she'll have a lead on Marcus too. After that I'm not sure."

"Cy, if it were anyone else but you I'd be seeking an involuntary commitment, you know that right", she asked.

"I do", I said, "and I am truly grateful that you believe me. I still have moments where I doubt everything and I was there."

She placed her palm on my chest and looked up at me with those beautiful eyes. "You'll figure it out Cy", she told me, "you always do". For a brief moment the urge to kiss her was so strong. I could tell it's what she wanted. In that moment I wanted it too. But I didn't have a lot of friends and sex ruins friendships. I hugged her and rested my chin on top of her head. Holding her close I could believe it, if only for this rare moment. Standing here holding my friend

I did something I almost never did. I prayed. Not to any one being but rather to anything that was good in the universe. I prayed for answers. But I prayed even more that I wouldn't screw this up.

Chapter Nine

After Clara left there was no way I was going to be able to sleep. My mind was spinning and I was having trouble centering myself. So, what does any intelligent person do when they can't think? Go for a run in freezing temps, of course. What could possibly make more sense? I bundled up enough to keep complete hypothermia at bay, but not enough that I couldn't move at all, and headed out. It was a delicate balance between movement and waddling. I run naked, which means no headphones or distractions. But just try to tell people that you run naked and see the looks you get. It's a fun time.

The wind was brutal as the weak sun tried to warm an earth perma-locked in its frigidity. The cold air scorched my lungs as I started the first mile. I had discovered years ago that if my mind was all twisted up, physical movement was sometimes the cure. Something about being able to shut my brain off and let my body take over gave my mind time to unravel its own Gordian Knot. I thought of it as an escape from my brain's own bullshit, but I'm sure some psych somewhere had whole studies on it. They always do. You'll have to forgive me. I'm a firm believer in mental health and counseling. But having dated a mental health counselor after the divorce and seen what she tried to do to me and how she tried to twist me up, I had a rather bad taste in my mouth about them overall. It's personal bias, just ignore me.

Mile one stretched behind me as I circled into a residential neighborhood. The area was mostly newer homes mixed in with old. A few years ago the little town of Kernersville had a population explosion and growth had taken off way faster than anyone had expected. I loved running through these neighborhoods. My time as a cop and medic here had left me with some bad memories but with friendships with many of the residents. Usually I would see at least one or two friendly faces anytime I ran. Today was an exception though. The cold air and biting wind had people firmly entrenched in their homes. No one wanted to deal with this weather when they could be inside and warm. Truth be told, neither did I, but my mind and I are not friends sometimes.

Something about the air today was bothering me. Yeah, it was cold, but it had a weight to it. The air itself felt ominous. I knew air didn't have a mind or feelings, but everything had a vibe that was slightly malevolent. You know how you'll walk through a place and just have that feeling that you're not welcome? That if you stay you may never walk out again? It was like that. Or maybe I was the only one that ever felt like that? If so, I'm weirder than I think I am.

As I turned right on Nelson St. heading towards Church St. I thought I saw the air shimmer out of the corner of my eye. Faint, hardly noticeable really. It was probably a trick of the cold air. Yeah, that was it. Rationalization is the tool of sanity. I was drawing closer to what I thought I saw when I heard something skittering along the asphalt behind me. My instincts kicked in before my mind could process the sound and I went from a full jog, or forced waddle depending on how you look at it, to having stopped and pivoted to face whatever was behind me. Hands raised to protect myself and feet in a firm combat stance I was ready to fight.

And there was nothing there. Leaves blew across the asphalt. I quickly realized that the sound I had heard came from the leaves rustling in the wind. And now I was standing on the side of the road in a fighting stance feeling like a complete idiot. I wasn't jumpy. Nope, I wasn't jumpy at all. I was prepared for whatever came. Yeah, that was it. Hoorah... yeah right.

I started to relax. Didn't want the neighbors calling the cops about the crazy man trying to fight leaves. I was breathing heavily from the run and the adrenaline. I felt foolish. What was wrong with me? Getting scared by leaves of all things. I mean, yeah, I had been attacked twice by monsters in the same number of days but should that make me a basketcase? Ok, good point.

It was cold and my mind was playing tricks on me, that was all. I thought I might as well take a shortcut and head back home before I waddled into traffic or something. I turned back to my route, willing warmth and movement into my frozen legs. And all I could see was teeth. Hundreds of jagged yellowed teeth were surging towards my face in a bad imitation of a teenage make out session. The circular mouth pulsated causing green drool to fall from the black oozing tongue. I couldn't see what the mouth was attached to because it was coming at me too fast. The thing's breath was like sewage. I fell backwards on my ass as its spittle peppered my face. The putrid maw slammed shut where my head had been seconds before. I was sure I wouldn't have had a face had I not performed such a graceful tactical retreat. A green ooze-like drool flew through the air above my head.

I scrambled backwards out of the road and into someone's yard. A few feet from me I could see that where the shimmering illusion had been was now a six foot oval void hovering mid air. Nightmarish screams poured from the darkness and the inside of the portal surged like an oily womb. Dark gray tendrils of energy snaked from inside the void and dissipated into the air around it. I snapped my gaze back to Teethzilla as I started scrambling backwards, trying to create distance between myself and another improbability.

The thing roared, its voice a high pitched shriek that made me nauseous. The sound wasn't just an assault on the ears but on sanity itself. Really seeing it for the first time was just as bad as the sound. It stood about eight feet tall, its skin a pasty white beige. It was a color only found on the corpse of someone who had suffered a sick lingering death. A color of waste and decay and the sadness of the infirmities of death. The beast's chest was corded with muscles that moved in weird patterns under its flesh. Its limbs were thin but splayed from the elbows and knees down into long articulating claws that looked more like scythe blades. Its face was mostly mouth with what looked like six tiny eyes on either side of that piranha shaming mouth. A megalodon would have been proud of those teeth!

My continued scrambling had backed me into a set of wooden steps and I just kept climbing backwards. Four paw drive didn't have anything on my backwards crab crawl and sprawl up those steps. I couldn't even think about getting to a solid fighting stance or a good position as the thing was stomping after me as fast as I could crawl. All the gerbils in my head seemed to be locked into the flee for your lives protocol instead of the fight for your life programming I had been installed with by Dear Ol' Uncle Sam. Damned software updates.

Slowly penetrating through the mental fog of terror and sheer nope that was my mental process I could hear a woman's voice yelling from beside me. I looked to my right to tell the woman to run and saw old Ms. Agnes. She was probably about eighty but looked and acted like she came over with the original Viking explorers and had just decided to stay. She was a short woman with a shock of pure white hair, a sweet smile, and always wore bright simple farmers dresses and an old sweater.

But she wasn't smiling now. She was angry. I had expected fear. Terror would have been reasonable, but not anger. She charged towards the steps of her porch with as much aggression as the tooth fairy's fetish date had charging towards me. She reached in her pocket and pulled out a closed fist. As the beast started to step onto the first step it froze. All its forward momentum ceased like it had hit a brick wall. Ms. Agnes laughed and threw a handful of powder at the beast. The powder seemed to shimmer as it moved softly through the air. When the powder touched it, the beast screamed. That's the only word I have for it. It screamed in a hundred empty voices, so loud I thought my ears would bleed.

Shrieking, it turned and sprinted back towards the seething void. The void began to close as it drew nearer and the beast just managed to fling itself through as the air sizzled and popped. The void vanished, or closed somehow, and the monster escaped in it or maybe through it. I lay on my back, gasping and wondering what I had gotten myself into now.

Before I could overthink it Ms. Agnes walked over and looked down at me. It was probably a strange sight really. Big muscular tattooed guy lying on his back guppy gulping on her front porch. Steam was rising off my body and my breath was creating small tornadoes in the cold air. I felt like my lungs were going to implode. Adrenaline is great in the moment, but the aftercare is a bitch.

"Well, come on in", she said. She turned her back and walked into her house like nothing had happened. You gotta love little old ladies in the South. Nothing much gets to them. Not even slavering demons from beyond.

Still lying on my back I managed to croak, "what was that"?

"Hot powder boy", Agnes said as she walked through her screen door. "Hot powder will send such things running".

Since that answer didn't make any more sense than anything else I went with it. If I was crazy I might as well embrace it. Do they make straight jackets in gigantor sizes? And just how does one find grippy socks in size fourteen? Maybe there'd be pudding? At least the part of my brain in charge of all quips and smart assery was working fine.

I heaved myself up off the porch noticing all kinds of fun new aches and pains. What a wonderful day in the neighborhood!

I stumbled the first few steps but managed to walk through the screen door instead of falling through it. Just inside the door was a simple warm living room with an old seventies style tv against one wall. A couch and two armchairs were positioned around it. All the furniture had old crocheted blankets draped along the backs. The kind someone's grandmother would drape over you during a nap.

I could hear Agnes moving in the kitchen just down the hall so I headed that way. As I walked in I was a little stunned by just how light and warm the room was. Old countertops and worn cabinets lined the walls. A beautiful real wood dining table sat just in the middle, its surface worn with years of love and use.

"Have a seat and I'll bring you some tea", Agnes said as she worked over the kettle on the old gas stove. "I suppose you have questions".

She said it as a statement instead of a question but I answered anyway. "Yes ma'am, I do". I was tired of nothing making sense and I really needed information. Was I crazy? Had I slipped off into the realm of a 1960's TV show? Nothing made sense anymore, but then nothing ever really did to me. Life was just a long stretch of highway at night, and my headlights were too dim to see the road. I needed help.

Agnes brought two steaming mugs to the table and sat down. I could see she wasn't going to say a thing until I joined her so, being the gentleman that I am, I sat across from her at the table with only a few minor groans. Agnes smiled a little as she watched me struggle to sit without whimpering. She gently passed me a mug of something that smelled like all the good memories of home I'd probably never had. I gingerly sipped the scalding tea and waited patiently. One does not rush little old southern ladies. They have frying pans and know how to use them.

"I'm going to tell you a lot of things, it will be up to you as to whether you choose to believe them or not", Agnes said. "Suffice to say, I've been here for longer than you might think. This isn't the first time I've met one of those bugaboos".

"Bugaboos, ma'am", I asked.

"Don't you play cop with me young man", Agnes said. "Call them what you will, that one wanted your hide boy".

"Sorry, ma'am", I said. Baby Bhuddas left nut, I was turning into a twelve year old here. Reverting to prior childhood traumas perhaps? There was something earthy and ancient about Agnes I hadn't noticed before. A vitality and a youthful sexuality dimmed but not dead within her aged frame. Not yet the crone, but definitely the lady. It was just a gentle power and confidence most women didn't have anymore. No criticism, men weren't any better. Times change and the lessons of past generations are lost.

"You don't need to ma'am me either", she said, "though I enjoy the courtesy". She smiled at me. "Guess I shouldn't have called you 'young man' if I didn't want to be called ma'am", she said with a laugh. Her laugh seemed to brighten the room. It was the kind of sound that would've turned heads at parties and made men holding High Balls turn and stare.

"Thank you", I said and omitted the 'ma'am'. "And thank you for helping me out with that......thing", I said not really knowing what to call it.

"I don't really know what to call that one either", she said. It was almost like she read my mind. "The dark hole in the air? The void? Those are called Nihils".

"Nihil, like Neitzche and his philosophical stance", I asked.

"Ah, you read philosophy, I like that", she said and gave me a gamin grin. Oh man, was she flirting with me? I mean, I'm all for grandma getting her groove on, but I didn't know how to act. "In a sense, very like Neitzche's Nihil, but an actual physical phenomena instead of the philosophical thought that all life is meaningless".

"Ok", I said and sipped my tea while I tried to think through what she had said. I drew a blank and sipped. Sooner or later there would be a context clue I could grab. Surely there would.

"Nihils are voids in our reality. Or, think of them as portals from a place of absolute negative or absolute positive that bridge into a world of absolute neutrality. Our reality is made up of neither absolute order nor entropy, but of a sliding scale between". Agnes paused and gently blew on her tea before continuing. "As our reality is in flux and not polarized by either absolute, entities from either world will sometimes try to break through. What you saw out there, is one of those entities".

"Why do they come here", I asked. "Wait, why did it come after me", I narrowed the question. I had a feeling the first would have been more than my fragile mental gerbils could handle. I couldn't afford for them all to develop alcoholism.

"Both are very good questions", Agnes said. "But you're smart to limit it". She chuckled again and winked at me. "Simply put, they're coming after you because you're someone who can stop them. Didn't you wonder why that old preacher came to see you in your kitchen? Didn't you wonder why your grandmother came to you?"

"How do you know about Marcus", I asked.

"Marcus has been stirring up trouble and trying to open the nihils for years", she said. "He sought you out for the same reason he sought out your grandma. He thinks your family has some secret to opening the nihils and setting darkness and entropy free upon our reality".

"But, why would anyone want to do that"I asked, rocking back in my chair. It didn't make any sense. Wasn't the world bad enough already? I mean, we already had the IRS and survived Glam Rock. Wasn't that enough?

Agnes sighed a gentle little sigh and watched me through her eye lashes. She had been toying with her mug and watching the ripples in the tea. "Haven't you ever been so angry you could destroy the world", she asked.

I flashed back to a dark night, a flipped mini van. "Yeah", I whispered, "I've been that angry".

"Marcus was a preacher", she said. "A Reverend, as they called them. One night some strangers were staying in the Salem district. Marcus had been called over to the township of Waughtown to minister to some folks. His wife and two daughters were killed while he was away. There aren't many records of it. The only account comes from the Sheriff of the time who said the bodies were found in the house slaughtered like sheep. The next week there was an entry in the town chronicle of two men and three women hanged and their bodies burned. I heard stories that Marcus's family was taken because he was a reverend and used by some folks who thought they had power to try and open a nihil of their own. Thought slaughtering the family of a holy man would add a little extra magic to their madness".

Agnes stopped looking at me and gazed into her tea. The entire house was silent. It was so still I could hear her breathing. Nothing else moved. Not the tick of a clock, not a drip in the faucet. It was silent and still as though the house itself was holding its breath. I held still too, waiting for the rest of the story.

"Old Marcus, he went mad. Became obsessed with the strangers and what they were trying to do. Marcus thought that if he could complete their ritual, he would bring his family back."

"He who looks into the Abyss and all that", I asked, quoting Neitzche.

"Exactly", she said.

"But that's not how it works, is it", I asked. "I mean, if the nihils are portals to absolute evil, then how would he bring back his family?"

"Ah", Agnes said and looked at me. She had that look like she wanted to give me a gold star, or get me naked, I couldn't tell. "Remember, nihils are just portals. But they are portals to places of absolute evil, or absolute good. Marcus has been searching for so long that he's lost sight of anything you or I would call rational or sane. I think that Marcus believes he can change the flow of a nihil from evil to good and find a bridge to his family."

"Wait", I interrupted. "You said Marcus had been summoned to the township of Waughtown from Salem. But that's impossible".

"Oh, why is that", Agnes asked me.

"Because that all became Winston Salem over a hundred years ago", I said.

"Closer to two hundred years when you look at it", she said.

"But humans don't live that long", I stated. There was no way Marcus was that old.

"Who says Marcus is still human", Agnes said with absolutely no kindness or warmth in her voice.

I stopped. Full halt, thou shalt not pass "go" or collect two hundred Hobbits. I had seen Marcus do a lot of impossible things. So why was it an impossible thought that he was something other? Something that maybe started as human and changed. Mutated? Oh man, hopefully not evolved, I did not want that to be humanity's final form.

"So, what do I do now", I asked her.

"Stop him, just like your grandma tried to do. Stop him from opening more nihils. Stop him from destroying our reality."

I sat for a few minutes processing before my brain clicked over. Agnes watched me work through it. Fair enough, stop the bad guy. I'd been doing that for years. Three cheers for solid ground. I could do this. Finally, a real direction!

"Ok", I said. "I think I've got it. Thank you for the tea and for explaining some of this to me. I'm just glad I haven't gone crazy".

"No Cy, you haven't gone crazy. You just have new responsibilities."

I started towards the front door with Agnes following me out. I stood on the porch for a minute looking at where the nihil had been. I shook my head. The only sign that anything had happened were some marks on the lawn where I had crab crawled for my life. I turned back to face Agnes.

"Take this", she said and handed me a little jar of powder and a slip of paper.

"What's this", I asked, holding the jar up to look at it.

"The jar is Hot Powder in case you need it", she said with a grin.

"And the paper", I asked.

"That's my phone number in case you get lonely", she said with a giggle and shut the door.

Sigh.

Chapter Ten

I managed to hobble home and shower. I knew I'd be sore as hell tomorrow so I stood under the jets and let them beat along the planes of my body. The sight of the water streaming out of my beard and down my stomach and legs became mesmerizing as I soaked up every degree of heat the shower could give. I never really noticed the scars or tattoos anymore. It was just my skin. It was just me. Even if I didn't know who that was anymore. I got out of the shower and dried off. Looking into the desolation of my fridge I realized I couldn't survive on ketchup and a half pack of bratwurst of questionable age. Looked like it was time for a trip to the grocery store.

I checked the voicemail on my phone expecting more calls about my car's extended warranty. As I was naked and slightly chilly I padded into the bedroom to find clothing more appropriate to my sense of style. Instead of a stranger, a warm sultry voice played out of the phone's speaker.

"Mr Magnus, I would like to extend you an invitation to my new club", the recording of Lila's delicious voice said. "I believe you know it well. Come to Heller tonight or tomorrow night so that we can talk. I look forward to seeing you here."

That stopped me. Lila owned Heller? Lila owned a BDSM club? I knew it had gone downhill after I left but when did she buy it? Heller had started as a few friends with similar interests wanting a safe space to be themselves. My ex-wife and I had been heavily involved in the founding of Heller and in growing it. A lot of people would probably think involvement in a club like that would have hurt our marriage but it helped. Just because we were kinky didn't mean we had to sleep with others. The few times we'd had problems we had even utilized a marriage counselor we knew through Heller to get back on track. It had been a community for us. Questions about Lila owning the place pounded through my head. Old cops hate questions, we have to answer them. Usually at cost.

I chose dark blue jeans, a black hoodie over a black t-shirt and black combat boots for the evening. Black leather coat and various items of lethality went on last. I debated bringing Lila's knife and finally incorporated it in an old spine sheath in the leather jacket. I'd had the coat for a long time and some modifications were just necessary.

Fully dressed I decided to head out. There was a small grocery near my apartment that would have everything I needed. I preferred small local establishments. I could say all kinds of things about supporting local businesses, which was important, but it was also just easier to watch the patterns and know who belonged and who didn't. It seemed like a simple thing, but it would keep me alive. Paranoid, who me?

I made it to the grocery in the icy heart of night. Global warming my ass, I'd swear I passed a polar bear on the drive in. It was the kind of cold that could give a man a cryo vasectomy. Freezing, I locked the car and moved inside with a purpose. I wasn't running but I was considering it.

Walking inside was always a homey experience. The inside of the store was warm and inviting. None of those commercial store halogen bulbs here. Mr. Murphy ran a warm store with warm lighting. The inside always smelled like great food, usually because Mr. Murphy had made himself a little kitchen in the back where he could cook for himself on long days. Mrs. Murphy would bring stew or ingredients the store didn't have and stop by after work so they could enjoy dinner together. It was that family owned dream so many have and few accomplish. I noticed they had a new cashier, a pinched faced younger woman who looked like she'd had it rough and had been just as rough right back. I nodded to her as I grabbed a basket and headed to the isles.

After a few minutes of perusing, something started bothering me. I couldn't put my finger on it at first. You ever have something nagging at you but you just can't figure out what it is? Yeah, like that. I took a couple of deep breaths and let my mind go. The brain wants to focus on the fact that it can't figure something out. But if you work counterintuitively and just let go, focus on nothing, everything suddenly comes into focus. It was an elegant example of "free your mind and your ass will follow".

It was quiet. Not like no one was speaking. No, everything was deathly quiet. I couldn't hear anything in the shop. No one breathing or moving, no music or the jingle of the cash register. Utter silence. I eased my hand around behind my back to Lila's knife. Silence was the first clue that something was wrong. The lights suddenly dimmed and then flickered. Here we go, fight time!

"Excuse me young man", a voice said. I spun and started to draw the knife. Undead bastard wasn't going to get me! And I froze. All the sound returned and all the lights came back up. Oh shit. Standing in front of me was a harmless old lady. What kind of bullshit was this? She was even smiling at me.

"Could you please hand me those pickles", she said and pointed to the top shelf.

"I'm so sorry ma'am", I said and pulled the pickles off the shelf. "You just startled me".

"It's quite alright young man", she said. "My husband was the same way". She smiled at me again.

"I'm sorry for your loss", I said and meant it.

"Don't be, Delbert was a right bastard but I loved him anyway", she said. She reached up and patted my cheek. "Be careful tonight, I have a feeling", she said.

"I will ma'am", I said. She turned with a smile and walked off. I shook my head and went to finish my shopping. How had I stepped into the Twilight Zone? It wasn't my choice to end up here but here I was. Let's just hope no one yelled "Leeeeroy Jenkins", in the near future. I got everything I needed and went to the check out.

"Will this be all sir", the pinched faced lady at the checkout asked.

"Yes please", I said. "Where's Mr. Murphy", I asked.

"He took the night off", she said as she rang up the groceries. "He hired me two nights a week so he could have a break", she said. Her voice was wooden and emotionless. Odd but she did work retail. That'll kill your soul quick.

"And your total will be $67.50 sir", she said. I pulled four twenties out of my wallet and handed them to her. Our hands brushed as she took the money and her face changed. Her face flashed from a pinched faced hard worn woman to a mask of shadow. A pitch black mask of writhing darkness. I didn't exactly jerk my hand back but I probably didn't miss it by much either. She didn't notice, just counted out the change and handed it to me. I tried not to look spooked as I grabbed the two paper bags and headed out of the store.

The icy wind slapped me as I noticed a lone figure standing by my car. Let's see, cloaked in shadow, dressed all in black, standing ominously. Yep, had to be Marcus.

"Good evening Mr. Magnus", the figure said. Yep, see, Marcus. It was like I was psychic or something. Only my radar was stuck on crypt keeper weirdos instead of anything useful.

"Good evening Marcus", I said and moved to put the groceries in the back seat. No need to worry about them going bad in this cold.

"Did you see something", Marcus asked.

"Other than you trying to look scary and probably getting hypothermia doing it", I asked back.

"Come now, what did you think of the new cashier", he asked and gestured towards the storefront.

"I think I'm tired of all your games", I said. Marcus, Lila, all of it. They needed to pack up this weirdshitapalooza and get back on the road. I was going to pack up my toys and play in a different sandbox with the normal kids. Even if a few did have special helmets.

"You think this is all a game", he asked. I could see he had about had it with my shit as well. Which was interesting since I hadn't even begun to give him a rasher of shit. But I was willing and oh so able.

"I think you are one creepy fuck who keeps throwing me to the monsters and I've had enough of your Blue Falcon ass", I said.

"Blue falcon", he asked. He had turned his head to the side. Clearly I was speaking a foreign language.

"It means Buddy Fucker", I explained. It did no good to insult him if he didn't even get the insult.

"But we are not buddies Mr. Magnus", he said.

"No, we aren't". Damn but he had me there. Asshole. He looked behind me and I took a step back before looking as well. I wanted some space in case he decided to swing. The lights in the store had all been shut off and the clerk was leaving. She looked like she was in a hurry but who wouldn't be in this weather? Except, the shadows seemed to move around her as she walked to her car.

"You should follow her", Marcus said to me. I looked back to find him already getting into my car. How had he done that? I know I locked it. I got in behind the wheel and fell in behind the clerk's little gray sedan as she drove off. I kept six to eight car lengths between us and tried to slow down every time she made a turn. Following someone at night could be harder than in daylight because the shape of your headlights never changed and traffic usually wasn't as dense. We followed her for about fifteen minutes out towards Hwy 158. We were just about to reach the rural highway when Marcus spoke up.

"Pull over here", he said.

"At the nursing home", I asked.

"Yes that will be fine", he said.

"But we may lose her", I told him.

"Do not worry, I know where she is going", he said.

I pulled over and waited. Sure enough the little gray car crossed the highway and pulled into an empty lot. When I was a kid it had been a restaurant. Later it was a truck stop for a while before everything was torn down and it became just an empty lot. I had killed the headlights as we pulled over but it didn't look like the clerk had noticed us. She sat in her car for a minute before shutting off the engine and getting out. Her breath fogged the air and she appeared to be speaking. From a pocket she drew a small knife and sliced her arm. From out of nothing, there suddenly sat a small gothic church or temple. But it wasn't the temple of any god I knew. The front columns were shaped like decayed corpses and the walls looked like stone shaped from flayed flesh. The roof dripped a black thick substance to the ground.

"What the hell is that", I demanded.

"Just watch", Marcus said. The clerk went back to her car and pulled a small wrapped bundle from her back seat. She seemed to be struggling with it as she shouldered the door to the "church" and made her way inside.

"What the hell is that", I demanded again.

"That is a node. A place where realities touch. Where beings from other dimensions can mingle with this one",

Marcus said. "And where humans can enter those same dimensions if they are powerful enough".

"Doesn't look like a nihil", I said.

"And how do you know that term", Marcus asked.

"Lila", I answered. Damned if I'd rat on Ms. Agnes.

"That woman will lead you to a bad end. She is treacherous", Marcus said while watching the church.

"Pot Kettle", I said and Marcus snorted.

"That is not a nihil. And yet it is all the same. Nihil's are portals yes, but they are so much more. The larger and more powerful the portal, the thinner the walls between realities, the greater the place that can hold them. Think of them like embassies or large churches. The larger they are the more powerful."

"So that's bad", I asked.

"Bad does not total what that is. But in your words, yes, it is bad, though not the worst", Marcus said. He wouldn't look at me.

"What's worse", I asked. Yeah, I was baiting him, so what?

"Pray, Mr. Magnus, that you never find out", Marcus said. He glared at me with eyes so clear I thought I could see hell through them. Not the hell of the religion of your choice, but the hell of a soul so tormented there was no saving it.

"Right, so, what do we do about it", I asked.

"You, not we, should investigate", he said.

"Investigate it, right", I sat and looked at the church of flesh, stone, and horror for another minute. "You wouldn't happen to have a small yield nuke somewhere would you", I asked hopefully.

"I'm afraid not", he said.

"Great, yay for the good guys", I said. I thought for a minute about calling Lila for back up. No way could I call Sam or Clara. They'd be outgunned. I had worked alone a lot. Some cops never did but deputies really did subscribe to the "One Ranger, One Riot" philosophy. I had my handgun on my hip and my Mossberg Shockwave in the back, but I had an overwhelming feeling guns weren't going to help me here. Maybe a sword? I could tote around a katana and pretend to be a Highlander? Nah, I'd need a battle axe and those things were way expensive. Don't ask. Ok, time to nut up or shut up. I got out of the car and could swear I could hear a phantom voice on the wind scream, "Leeeroy Jenkins".

Chapter Eleven

I checked both ways as I crossed the highway. Trucks barreled along this stretch all the time without really looking for pedestrians. It really could be a dark and lonely highway. It wasn't like I could really sneak up to a gothic horror church in the middle of the night that no one else could see. So I strolled casually like I owned the world. As I approached the double doors I could see that the figures carved into the columns weren't actually stone. They stood on either side of the door with legs trembling and their arms extended above their heads straining to hold the covering over the door upright. Dark liquid dripped slowly from the eaves and smelled like septic bowels that had a gangrenous ulcer. As I approached I could hear muffled cries and realized that the figures' mouths were sewn shut so they couldn't scream. I passed between them and to the doors. There were no knobs, just a push style bar on either side made of human femur bones. I went to push the bar and a human eye popped open where a peep hole or greeter hole should have been. I jumped but didn't scream. The eye tracked to me and looked me up and down before closing again. The door swung open without me touching it. Well, someone knew I was here and had invited me in. That was both a good thing and a really bad one depending on how I wanted to look at it.

I stepped inside and just to the side of the door so I wouldn't be silhouetted against the night. The door swung quietly closed, sealing me in. It took a minute for my eyes to adjust to the weird lighting. Dark gray candles lined half the surfaces in the church. All of them glowed with a black burning flame that somehow still emitted light. A large chandelier made of bone and held together by sinew hung overhead covered in the same candles. To my right sat an old grandfather clock made of flesh. The hands of the clock were tongues. I looked closer and the clapper in the center appeared to be a kidney. I so did not want to hear this bell toll. I stood still and looked around more fully.

The pulpit appeared to be made of intestines which were writhing and pulsing as if waiting for some dark sermon. There was a large stained glass window to my right at the center of the church. The glass, or whatever it was, showed a scene of indescribable torment. Light streamed softly through the window and lit what should have been the baptismal font. I could see black liquid writhing and churning hungrily inside the font.

The cashier stood topless in front of the font. Her hair lay stringy around her shoulders and her bare back was criss crossed with scars and burns. She was muttering something but it was either too low for me to hear or in a language I didn't know. She held out the cloth wrapped bundle with both arms. The bundle was struggling like it was not having a good time. As it writhed the head of a puppy emerged from the bundle. The puppy took one look at the writhing pool and bit the woman's hand. From the screams and the spurt of blood I'd say she had just lost three, maybe four, fingers.

"Oh hell no", I said before I realized what I was doing. I charged towards the woman. She turned to face me and started to drop the dog. Her face was pale and shocked as blood spurted from her stumps. "You can hurt as many humans as you like. Humans are shitty. But you do not hurt dogs", I bellowed into her face. I snatched the writhing bundle out of the air just before it hit the font and slapped the woman with all my strength. Her head rocked back and she fell screaming into the writhing pool. I literally pimp-slapped the woman into the pool. She screeched and writhed trying to escape but the dark liquid climbed over her body, sucking her down into it. I shouldn't have done it. Looking back I almost felt bad about it later. I raised my boot and kicked her square in the face, finishing her descent into the pool. I watched the liquid fill her mouth as she tried to scream before it covered her eyes and finally the last of her. It swallowed her and suddenly lay still. Not one ripple or eddy. I pulled the rags off the puppy and checked it over. It was definitely a boy. But he seemed fine. I looked deep into his eyes and felt a connection, a click within my soul that was almost audible. He licked my face and I knew this dog was different. I just didn't know how.

Sibilant whispers began echoing throughout the church. The gossiping voices of a hundred throats all speaking at once filled the hall of horror and decay. The pulpit collapsed to the floor and the intestines all writhed off in different directions. Sentient slimy snakes of their own devisement. The altar behind where the pulpit had been began to morph into the shape of a throne. As it did it grew outwards from the wall encroaching on the small space until it was maybe three feet from the baptismal font on the far side from me. The walls and roof shuddered around me as the throne grew closer. After several seconds the movement stopped and the entire church seemed to creak and groan quietly. I quickly bent and set the puppy behind me. Hopefully he didn't wander off until I had dealt with this. I turned back to the throne to see a figure sitting upon it regally. One leg thrown over an arm of the throne, hands steepled in front of him. He was dressed in some type of flexible black armor, lean and fit. I couldn't tell if he wore a mask or if it was his face but from brow to above his lips was bone with sharp cheekbones like points. Below the nose dark black skin formed a smiling mouth and perfect chin. Sitting on top of his head was a crown of bones sharpened to spikes. He smiled at me and his dark eyes were intent. This was someone that liked to toy with their prey.

"Well, well, well, who do we have here", the figure asked. From the darkness I saw two dark robed figures step up on either side behind the throne. They were enshrouded in their robes so deeply I could barely make out their shapes. They stood silent and still behind their king.

"Name's Cy, and you", I asked. All balls, no brains, that's me.

"Cy, Cy, Cy,", the figure singsonged. Hissing echoes gently came back to me mocking the parody he was making of my name.

"I am Loros, one of the Shadow Kings", he said.

"One of the what", I asked.

Oh dear", he said. "Do you not know of The Shadow Kings?"

"Can't say that I do", I said. "But I'm kinda new here so..."

"Ah, I see", he said. "Then allow me to help you. Throughout what your kind are calling the Shadow Lands, that's a dreadful name you know, there are several different planes or dimensions. Each one has its own king. I am Loros the Triumphant and I am king of one of these dimensional planes".

"Pleasure to meet you", I said. It wasn't but what else should I say? Fuck off? Maybe.

"I can see we shall have to develop a better PR campaign in your dimension over the next eon or so", he said more to himself than to me.

"So, I'll just be going", I said and turned to grab the dog and get out of Dodge.

"One moment please", he said. Everything stilled. I wasn't even sure I was breathing. I turned back to Loros.

"You are in my dimension at the moment and I would appreciate the courtesy of a word please", he said. It was framed as a request but somehow I didn't feel like it was one.

"Ok" I said simply. I had the feeling that this could go bad at any time so maybe humoring him would get me out of a fight.

"You have had contact with a being who calls himself Marcus, yes", Loros asked.

"Um, yeah, I have", I wasn't sure if admitting that was a good thing or not.

"And you have met the Lady Lila, correct", he asked again.

"I have", I said. In for a penny, in for a pound. Wait... bad thought, at least standing in this place.

"Just this then. You stand between two poles or frameworks. Be careful who you choose to follow. You may liken them in your mind to moral good or evil but neither is purely such. Be very careful the path you choose and who you choose to walk it with. I assure you, if you choose poorly, I will see you lying dead on the floor of my temple", he told me. I carefully thought about this for a moment. Yes, I really listened.

"Thank you for your advice", I said. "I have been thinking along those lines myself".

"Then may I give you a gift, a gift I swear I mean only to help you", he said. "My word as a King of the Shadow Lands".

"Yeah, ok, sure", I said. I didn't know if his word had any value, but why not?

"The Lady Lila gave you a blade", he said. "May I see it".

"Sure", I said, though I really didn't feel sure about it. How had he known she gave me a knife? Hell, was this the king the zala had mentioned, intending to destroy my reality? Questions, questions.

He stood from his throne as I pulled the knife from inside the jacket. I flipped it, held it by the blade, and extended it to him. The figures behind the throne moved slightly, their robes making a gentle rustling sound, then stilled once more. Bodyguards maybe. As Loros moved closer I realized he was like seven feet tall. Holy crap! He took the knife gingerly and examined it. Blue script flared to life on one side of the spine. He turned the knife over and examined the second side. After a moment's thought he pricked a finger with one of his own nails and then etched a design in the blank side of the blade. Purple fire burned along the design as he etched it in with his fingernail. I'd hate to be his manicurist. After examining his work for a moment he handed the blade back to me.

"This may help you. And if it does not, it will surely upset that ghoul Marcus", he said with a predatory smile. I took the knife and smiled back.

"Oh, and thank you for ridding us of that one", he said and gestured to the baptismal font. "Anyone who would harm an animal is not the kind of person we want around". He turned and walked towards the throne. As he did he dissolved in mid air. Seconds later his attendants did likewise. Except the one on my right didn't fully dissolve. Two black tendrils shot from it at the last moment heading for my chest at amazing speed.

From somewhere behind me a full sized demon of a dog or wolf sprang from the darkness and attacked the shadow tendrils. Teeth like bear traps snapped and rended, ripping the tendrils to shreds. They fell to the floor and dissolved. The wolf or dog or demon huffed and turned to look at me with glowing red eyes. Then it shifted, returning to the shape of the puppy. What the hell? I feel like I ask that a lot. Do I ask that a lot these days?

"What kind of puppy chow do you eat", I asked the puppy. He whined a little, pissed on the floor, and then trotted happily over to me. I picked him up and headed out of this phantasmagoria. Looks like I had a new friend.

Chapter Twelve

It was almost dawn when I stumbled out of Loros' church. I looked around in the pre-dawn light but of course, Marcus was nowhere to be seen. Shocker there. I carried the puppy back to my car and headed home. My apartment complex had a no dogs policy so I knew I'd have to sneak him in. I stuffed him in my coat until we got inside. Maybe we could keep each other from freezing? I got us inside and set him down on the floor. He immediately started sniffing and investigating everything. I got him some water and tried to figure out something for food. I finally gave him a small hunk of hamburger pulled apart so it wouldn't hurt his stomach. After he was bloated and nodding off we went to bed.

I was standing in a park. Kids' playground equipment stood neatly and unused. The grass was well manicured and the play sand had even been raked. That was my first clue. There wasn't a park anywhere this nice. Blue skies gleamed overhead and a gentle breeze blew through the area. But my dreams weren't usually this nice. From the tree line I heard a branch snap. I looked up to see a young girl in a white dress riding my dog. Well, the large frightening version of my dog anyway. The girl held her severed head under her left arm like a child would hold a basketball. Yep, now this looked more like one of my dreams. If it didn't rip my heart out and crush my soul, was it a Cy dream?

"Hello, Cy", the little girl said.

"Hi", I said or maybe whimpered.

"I see you've met my friend", she said. The hound licked her face. Which was under her arm. She giggled.

"Yeah, except he doesn't look like this in my world", I said and gestured at him.

"He won't when you're not threatened. This is his true form. Most people will never see him, and the few who do will only see a normal dog", she said. "But if you are threatened, this is what they will meet". The hound huffed and sat beside the girl.

"So, what is he", I asked. Hey might as well. She was at least giving me straight answers.

"This is a Hellhound", she said.

"Like from blues music and myths", I said.

"Definitely like your favorite music, Cy", she said and giggled again. "But absolutely not a myth. They are guardians. This one will help protect you wherever you go. Never leave his side and you will be in a good place". The dog laid down, his head between his paws, and looked up at me.

"Trust his senses even when you do not trust your own", she said and gave me a gentle smile. I felt a sharp sting on my earlobe.

I woke to find the puppy gnawing my earlobe and whining. Guess it was potty time. I took him outside and let him do his business. Several neighbors walked right past him and never noticed. Huh, guess the dream was right about that at least. Since I was going to have to get kibble anyway I bundled myself and the puppy up and went to the gym. When we got there I opened my gym bag and set the puppy inside nestled in my lifting belt. He looked back at me like I had lost my mind.

"Stay in the bag", I told him. He harrumphed at me and turned his head, ignoring me.

"Fine whatever", I told him. "Just don't get me kicked out". We went inside and I made my way past all the pretty people machines and treadmills to the very back. There was a powerlifters section very few people used. It wasn't a section for lightweights, pun intended. It was dim and filled with plate weights and barbells. Nothing fancy, nothing trendy, just old fashioned weights and sweat.

I loaded a barbell with a couple of forty-fives and started to warm up by deadlifting. After a few sets another person walked into the closed off section. I didn't pay any attention at first. I was zoned in on my lift.

"You did not come and see me last night", a warm voice said. I looked up, not sure if the person was talking to me. Lila was standing in front of me, dressed to workout, a water bottle in her hand. A sharp bark came from my gym bag. She looked down and the puppy poked his head out of the bag, one ear flopped over to the side. She knelt to examine him which gave me a great view of things I probably shouldn't be looking at. But it was an amazing view and I was only human. And if I didn't stop looking Lila was going to be... ahem... nose to nose with proof of what I was looking at. I took a step back and tugged my sweatshirt down hard.

"Sorry, I had something come up", I said. Which was probably a bad choice of words. She petted the puppy scratching him between the ears. He yawned and laid on his back, inviting belly rubs. Lila obliged.

"And this", she asked with a smile.

"I made a new friend", I said noncommittally.

"This I can see", she said and grinned at me. She was so beautiful. "A hellhound is not a pet, but a friend, so you have chosen the right way to think about him. For this, I can understand you not coming last night", she said.

"Hey, you did say I could come either night", I said and grinned at her. I took a step forward, invading her space slightly.

"And will you come see me tonight", she asked and pressed into me. Her full breasts pressed into my chest and I had no doubt she knew how I felt by how her pelvis pressed into mine.

"You keep doing this and I'll see you wherever you like", I said. She started to step away from me and I grabbed her firmly. I pulled her into me and roughly kissed her. She didn't even try to resist. We met with equal aggression, all tongue and teeth and passion. My hands roamed lower on her body and hers along my chest. Just as we were about to get to the part where we might need a room a gentle bark warned us of someone coming. We stepped apart and I pretended like I was panting from lifting the barbell. Lila took a long swig of water as the gym attendant walked through, said hello, and headed back up front. Meddling people, always in the way. I heard Lila snicker.

"Relax Cy, no need for frustration", she said.

"Isn't there", I asked and stared at her. She dropped her gaze.

"All in good time", she said and sat on one of the benches. "So, what is your plan about Marcus?" I groaned.

"Why do I have to have a plan about the soul sucking fun sponge", I asked.

"Because he is evil", she said. I thought back to Loros's comment last night.

"Neither you nor he are completely good or evil", I said. It didn't sound like me but it was definitely my thought.

"No, I suppose not", she said. "But in my list of evil I do not compare to him".

"That's probably true. But other than the fact that he keeps stalking me like a demented frat girl, how is he my problem", I asked.

"He will not leave you alone, you already know this", she said.

"Probably not, but you still haven't told me why you have such a beef with him", I said.

"He and I have a complicated history", she said.

"Like", I asked.

"LIke I should have killed him long ago", she said and rose. "Will you come tonight"?

"Yeah, I'll be there", I said.

"Good", she said. And with that she walked out. I stood fuming with a mixture of anger, frustration, and sheer horniness. That woman was going to drive me insane. If I wasn't already there, and I didn't think anyone was taking long odds on that. The puppy was gently snoring in my bag.

I finished my workout and grabbed a shower at the gym. A very cold shower. When I got out I found a text message from Sam asking if I could come by. I didn't have anything else to do so I told him I was on my way, grabbed my bag and faithful furrball, and headed out towards Winston. About fifteen minutes later I rolled up to a nice brick home off Pecan Ln in a nice subdivision full of cookie cutter houses. Sam's place stood out a little just because the houses were getting older and worn down, but Sam's looked clean and new. Sam liked to keep things neat. Not my kind of living but Sam and Betty had been here for years.

I pulled up in front of their brick home. Beautiful flowers were arranged all over the front yard and the lawn was neat. Not manicured or overdone, just neat. Sam liked order but he didn't overdo it. I got out of the car just as Nina, Sam's seventeen year old daughter, came out. Guess I had been gone longer than I thought. Pigtails and cardigans had been replaced by heavy make up and a full Goth ensemble. Which, let's be honest, I couldn't really say anything about.

"Uncle Cy", she shrieked and charged at me.

"Hello Girlie", I said and snatched her up in a huge bear hug.

"Put me down", she said but she was laughing. I set her back down on her feet.

"You're looking good", she said and gave me a look I wasn't really comfortable with from my goddaughter.

"So do you girl", I said. She stepped back and mock curtsied. When she did her bag popped open a little and I could see a book with a pentagram inside. Not my business.

She was at that age where she should be examining and experimenting anyway.

"Are you heading out", I asked.

"Yeah, I'm off to Cathy's", she blushed and giggled.

"And does Cathy have facial hair and know you have a psychotic uncle", I asked.

"Uncle Cy, really", she said.

"Just saying", I told her.

"Dad's waiting for you inside", she said and headed down the driveway. I went around to the other side of the car and got my bag full of puppy out of the seat. I walked up to the door and Betty, Sam's wife, met me there. She was beautiful with dark skin and bright eyes. I had seen her smile at people and watch them melt. She just had that aura about her.

"Cy, it's been too long", she said. She grabbed me and pulled me down to kiss my cheek.

"Get your hands off my wife", Sam's deep voice said from the living room.

"Get your wife's hands off me", I said and hugged her. "What are you afraid of, she'll finally realize she should have chosen me", I said. Sam began bellowing with laughter.

"You two", Betty said and swatted me gently as I released her. "Can I get you something Cy", she asked.

"Water, please ma'am", I asked.

"Of course", she said and headed to the kitchen.

"Come on in and sit down", Sam said. "I didn't think you'd ever come over".

"Yeah, I've been busy", I said

"Bullshit", he countered. "But it's ok".

"Nina has really grown up" I said, trying to change the subject.

"Brother you have no idea", he said. "Her last boyfriend almost had me calling you for an old fashioned ride". Meaning her last boyfriend had broken his daughters heart and he was looking to do violence. Couldn't blame him there.

"You got his address," I asked.

"Nevermind", Betty said as she walked into the room with a bottle of water.

"Thank you", I said as she handed me the water. "So, what did you need", I asked.

"Some real weird guys have been at the office asking about you", Sam said. "The suit and Ray Ban kind of guys".

"Feds", I asked. I wasn't in any kind of trouble, that I was sure of.

"They said they were but they had the flavor of alphabet soup guys", he said. The term alphabet soup referred to guys working for various government agencies who could be interchanged when they did something nefarious and illegal for dear old Uncle Sam stateside. They were faceless cogs in a machine so vast it was easy to get lost in. DIA, CIA, FBI, and probably PBS too for all I knew. But I wasn't important enough for those kinds of people to be interested in me.

"Well, today just keeps getting better", I said and leaned back in my chair. I wouldn't have noticed normally but my shirt must have opened at the neck and my amulet spilled out. Betty stood in one fluid motion, cold wind blowing off her like a gust in a storm. She started muttering under her breath and pulled a vial of something from her pants pocket.

She threw the contents on me and I realized it was salt. I sat motionless for a millisecond and then furious barking erupted from my gym bag by the door. As Betty moved in front of Sam in protection a tiny fur missile leapt from my bag and charged at Betty ready to commit puppy murder. Sam stood up behind Betty.

"Betty, what's the meaning of this", he asked.

"Stand back" she said and elbowed Sam in the gut. "Where's Cy and what are you"?

"It's me Betty, I swear", I said. I sat still, my arms held out with my hands open.

"Let me see the amulet", she said. She wasn't playing either. Sam was scary in his own right but not Betty. What was happening? I carefully pulled the amulet out and held it up for her to see. She stepped closer, obviously being super cautious. She got a good look at it and then looked deep into my eyes. Sam had bladed off behind her, not sure what to do or who to grab. Her eyes burned green for a moment and then she sighed.

"It's you", she said and collapsed on the floor. Sam and I both caught her as the yapping demon fiend ran back behind my chair.

"You've seen your grandmother", she asked.

"In a dream, or vision, yes. She came to me the other night", I said.

"Betty what's going on", Sam demanded.

"Just give me a moment", she said and patted Sam's face. The puppy decided he was brave again and came up to us as we knelt on the floor. He sniffed Betty and then licked her face. She laughed and petted him.

"Sam, help me sit up please", she said. He did but he looked really concerned.

"Have you seen a nihil yet Cy", she asked.

"Seen and been in one", I said. "Or at least a kind of one. It was not a fun experience. How do you know about them?"

"Sam", she said. "It's time to tell him".

"Betty, are you sure", he asked.

"I told you this day may come", she said.

"It's your choice", he said. I sat there waiting. Sometimes if you sat quietly you'd learn something.

"Cy, have you met a tall skinny man with dark hair? The kind who gives you the creeps every time he walks into a room. Athletic with lots of tattoos. They look tribal but they're not?" She was describing Marcus to a T.

"Yeah, Marcus the Crypt Keeper", I said. "He's a real asshole".

"Yes, Marcus, funny he still goes by that name", she said.

"How do you know him", I asked.

"Cy, you know everyone has things in their past they don't talk about right", Sam asked.

"Yeah, got some of that myself", I said thinking about my own redacted history.

"Well, just like you won't talk about your time in the military and after, Betty and I have things we don't talk about", he said. The lightbulb started to light up, just dimly. I kept quiet. See, not as dumb as I look.

"It's my history Cy, not Sams", Betty said. She eased herself up into a more comfortable position on the beige carpet. She was leaning back into Sam for support and maybe comfort.

"When I was seventeen I was involved with a cult. My family had been psychic or maybe even witches for as long as my great grandmother could remember. I don't even know what to call our abilities really. But I met a guy who said he could teach me things. I went to a few outtings, like most young people do when they're trying to find themselves, and I got sucked in. Everyone there was so supportive and they taught me things. Magicks that I thought were only fairy tales. It was family and community all in one. Marcus was the leader of the group", she told me. She looked so haunted. This was a trauma that had been with her for a long time.

"But things got dark. Marcus started teaching us about other dimensions. He wanted to open a gateway, what he called a...", I interrupted her.

"A nihil", I said.

"Yes, a nihil", she continued. "We never knew why he wanted to open one. He claimed that he wanted to help mankind. And we believed him. At least until", and she trailed off. I gave her a moment.

"Until", I gently prompted.

"Until he led one of the girls up to the altar during one of our gatherings. He slit her throat like a lamb. Her blood poured along the altar and a portal opened. It opened Cy", she looked so horrified.

"We all just stood there stunned. After it was over, a few of us started studying on our own. We wanted to stop him. We found out that nihils were actual metaphysical points where dimensions rubbed together. And certain energies could open them. But there was no real way to plot coordinates for which dimension you opened to. At least none we could find. Our research suggested that sometimes the nihils themselves could be sentient. That they could open themselves for their own purpose. I had met Sam at this point and I started drifting away from the group. Sam was so amazing", she said this and looked up lovingly at the big lunk.

"One night I was out with Sam at the old Drive In Theater in Walkertown. I'd gone to the bathroom and Marcus was waiting on me when I came out of the bathroom. He grabbed me, punched me, told me I was coming with him. That I would be the next sacrifice", she said. She looked so frail.

"I don't know how he knew, but Sam came charging up behind Marcus. Sam hit him with a tire iron. And kept hitting him", she said.

"I busted his head open with that tire iron and kept going Cy", Sam said. "I don't know what got into me, I just couldn't stop. I knew she was in danger. Felt it in the car. I couldn't stop myself", he told me. "I could see his brains on the ground, little chunks of hair wrapped around the tire iron and I just kept swinging. I was so ashamed but I knew if I didn't stop him he'd kill her."

"No one could have survived that Cy", Betty said. "He was dead." She started to cry a little and Sam held her tighter.

"So if you've met him, then he's back. You have to be careful, Cy", she told me. "He'll try to kill you too."

"Oh, I wouldn't worry about that", I told her. "I've got a few friends now", I told her and petted the puppy which had curled up in her lap. Friggin' traitor.

"Cy, I know why he wants you", she said. "I knew the day I met you. But nothing ever really developed so I thought I was mistaken", she said and paused. It was a long pause. I could tell she was trying to decide how to say it.

"The day Sam brought you home as a young rookie, I had a flash, a vision. You can control nihils Cy", she said this with a look of horror. "You can control them, create them, and destroy them. That's why he wants you Cy."

Chapter Thirteen

I left Sam and Betty feeling confused. Did everyone but me know about these things? Had I been in an intellectual vacuum? Was there some conspiracy? Did I need a tin foil hat? I mean, it's only a conspiracy theory until it becomes fact right? Who was writing this and why couldn't he have written me rich? I mean come on!

Since I had several hours to kill before Heller would open, I decided to visit Grandma Isabelle's grave. It had been a while and it was a quiet place to think. Maybe something would kick my brain into gear and help me process. It was a long drive from Pecan Ln to the other end of Reynolda. I did learn that the puppy adored Nine Inch Nails so we were able to bond on the drive. We hit Yadkinville Rd and turned into the cemetery. It was a huge place and Grandma Isabelle's grave was back off to the right and near the treeline. The old asphalt was warped and sat at odd angles due to years and tree roots. It was broad daylight but I kept seeing the shadows behind trees move. Normally I would have thought it was just an illusion. Now I wasn't so sure.

I found the right section and put the car in park. The puppy growled slightly and peered out the passenger side window. This was obviously not his vibe. I scooped him up and carried him to the grave. I sat staring at it for a minute or two. There really wasn't anything to feel creeped out about but I did. Little dude wasn't much better, he growled softly at the wind.

I was reading some of the headstones and cleaning up the little bits of debris all gravestones accumulate over time when I saw something weird. The names and dates on all the headstones were writhing. Each letter seemed to be climbing over themselves and dancing on the headstones. I looked back at Grandma Isabelle's headstone. It was the only one not doing it. I heard the tinkle of a small bell. Looking to my right I saw a small boy riding a tricycle through the grass between the graves. I stared at him for a moment wondering where his parents were. As he rode past me he faded. He just faded into nothing. I looked over towards the section reserved for veterans and saw an old soldier standing guard. But his uniform looked ancient. Like from World War One old. I had the realization that what I was seeing weren't living people, but the dead. I was seeing ghosts or maybe spirits. Something dark leapt from a tree branch and skittered along the ground. The puppy went nuts and leapt from my arms to give chase. A moment later he trotted back proudly like he had defended us from a ravening monster. Welp, I was well protected I thought with a snort.

I had brought fresh flowers so I put them out on Grandma's headstone and just stood staring for a few minutes. The puppy sat there with me, just waiting. After a few moments of standing in the wind and the silence I decided maybe asking for help wouldn't be such a terrible idea. I'd done worse.

"Grandma, I could really use some help here", I said to the wind.

"Weel, ye coulda done better on me headstone", a voice beside me said. I jumped but I didn't scream. I was proud of that. The puppy started huffing and I realized it was his version of laughter.

"Please don't do that", I said.

"Wee bit jumpy are you", she asked.

"As to your headstone, you'll need to talk to dad about that", I told her. She looked a row over where my dad's grave was located. She chuckled a little. I could only wonder if it wasn't the idea of talking to my dad about anything. If there was a more stubborn man on the planet, I'd never met him.

"So, what's on yer mind lad", she asked.

"I need to know if it's all true", I told her.

"I wish the answer was no, but it's true. This and so much more", she said.

"How", I asked simply.

"No one knows, I 'spect", she said. Her accent kept slipping between her younger and older years. "Me Ma told me about it when I was sixteen or so. I hunted monsters for years ye ken. Before I met your grandfather, rest his soul, I was even courted by a Prince of the Fae. It was a grand time. A scary time, but grand all the same." I smiled at her. I could see her dazzling some prince and leading him on a merry chase. She had been a handful when I knew her. Kept grandpa jumping. I could just imagine what a hell raiser she had been young.

"What happened there", I asked.

"With yon prince, ye mean", she asked.

"Yes", I said. I was curious.

"I met your grandda in London. He was a photographer during the war. I didn't know till later that he had been a spy as well. But I took one look at such a mighty man and knew no other 'twould do. And so I broke me courtship, and talked your grandda into settlin' in the mountains to make us a life.", She looked so wistful. I missed her a great deal.

"So is this my battle to fight", I asked her.

"Who ken say lad", she said. "I think that's a decision only you can make. I can tell you that if no one fights this battle, eventually things go out of balance. At some point there won't be any line between the planes, and that will end us all. Long ago the same happened, ye ken, and there was a great war between the planes. Hunters like me, and now you, were created to stop it from ever happening again. Our actions, sometimes great and sometimes evil, have kept the planes from crashing into each other for many a year. But you, you need to trust your own instincts and find your own path amongst the roses and thorns."

"Follow me lad, mayhaps I have something for ye", she said and started through the trees. We walked through the grass and trees with the puppy following along behind. We had reached a part of the cemetery so old the gravestones couldn't be read anymore. Years, maybe centuries of weather had eroded them to blank stone. I suddenly felt something. A hollowness in my stomach behind my navel. I told her about it.

"What yer sensing lad, is a nihil. A baby one. Whenever ye feel that, there'll be one nearby", she said. We were standing in front of two younger Oak trees and I suddenly realized that the closer we were to the nihil the younger she looked.

"Now reach out and tell me where ye think it is", she said. I immediately pointed to the ground between the two oaks and it became visible. A purple black hole writhing in the ground. Or on top of it.

"Now focus on what you're sensing and try to pull it to you", she said. I don't know how I knew what to do but I did. I focused on it and pulled, and it came. The nihil moved from between the oak trees and began to swirl around my feet. Tendrils of energy started climbing my legs. It felt good, whole, standing in that vortex. I felt alive. I could feel its energy whispering to me, warming me, calling me. It was one of the most seductive things I'd ever felt.

"Control it lad, lest it control ye", Grandma yelled at me. I focused all my will on it. Forced it to coalesce into a ball in front of me. It responded immediately. The energy pulsed and writhed, eager to do my bidding.

"Now tell it to go back where it came from", she told me.

"Go", I said to the ball of energy. It shrank into nothing with a soft sad pop. I felt forlorn for a moment. Like I had lost a friend. I looked back at Grandma Isabelle.

"Twas a man named Marcus who killed me lad. Ye've met him by now. Watch yer back", she said and started to fade.

"I thought you died in your sleep", I said.

"Marcus broke in late one night tryin' te steal yon necklace", she said pointing to my neck. "I stabbed him a good one, I did", she said with a smile.

"Did me little good though. As I lay dying he set the house on fire around me lad. He's an evil one", she said to me. My sudden rage broke white hot. Wind swept through the cemetery bending the trees. I was going to kill that bastard. Kill him permanently.

"Tut, tut. Yer rage does you justice but will nae help ye. Control it lad, until it's time to set it free", she said and faded away.

At that moment I didn't care what stood in my way, Marcus would die. And after I burned his body, I would salt the earth. Salt the fucking earth!

Chapter Fourteen

I had a lot of rage to burn off after that and nowhere to put it. Heller wouldn't open for another couple of hours and I didn't have enough time to go back to the gym. I took the puppy back to the car where we focused on deep breathing to heavy metal music. After about thirty minutes I stopped seeing red and started thinking again. I think it was about an hour of sitting with the puppy in my lap before I noticed the sunset. It was so beautiful. The strokes of orange and red amongst the purple of the clouds.

I lost myself in its beauty and found myself crying. Crying again for the loss of Grandma Isabelle. For the loss of so many I had loved and for the loss of all the people I had seen pass but never knew. Crying for myself and for Sam and Betty and so many others. Tears of sorrow, of rage, and of helplessness burned out of me as an offering to the beauty before me. As the last rays of light ebbed into night, I felt catharsis in a way I had never experienced. It was that moment of facing death and surviving. That clarity of shock that comes from great release and great rebirth. I felt as though I had passed through a crucible. Not the same kind as in boot, but a different sort. The kind that changed a man's soul forever.

I pulled myself together and headed to Heller. This would be fun. You'll forgive me if I don't describe where it is. Either you know or you don't. It keeps away the curious. I parked behind the old building and went to the entrance. You wouldn't know what it was from outside. It just looked like an older building. The rules were very strict and we had kept good relations with the neighbors, beat cops, and shot callers so that no one messed with the place or the members. I knocked three times, waited a pause, and knocked three more. The door opened. Most dungeons were way easier to walk into, but not Heller. Heller was a place of many rooms with open doors, each one locked tightly shut. I had set up the security myself. Vetting and ID checks were serious and if you didn't match, you left. Other places had problems with pervs or vanillas. Not us. I was proud of that. If you were having open sex, indulging your kinks, or were letting people inflict pain from minor to "oh my god" you had to be careful who you let in.

"I can't believe it", I heard as the door opened. A small man with black hair, maybe a hundred pounds soaking wet opened the door and knelt. It was Elias. Elias had wanted to be my sub from the moment I met him, but we just didn't jibe that well. Because I had said no so much, he had taken to trying to embarass me. I wondered if the games would continue? Time changes people, maybe it had changed him as well. No sub ever did this in real life, at least outside of a specific agreed on dynamic, so I always felt he was mocking me.

"Please get up, I'm not in the mood", I said to Elias and reached down to help him up. He flinched back.

"Mistress Lila gave me specific instructions for when you arrived sir", he said. He was being very specific and a little more respectful than normal.

"Is she your Domme now", I asked. I was genuinely curious. I liked the little guy, I just didn't want to top him.

"No, sir, I still serve Mistress Kalya, but Mistress Lila knew that I knew you. She asked specifically for me to assist you in any way possible", he explained.

"I'm glad you and Kalya are still together. Is this High Protocol", I asked.

"No sir, Mistress Lila just wanted specific things for you. Like a friendly face to guide you", he said with a smile. I smiled back. It really was good to be back home. And maybe it was fitting the Elias was the one who greeted me.

"Lead on then, please", I said. He stood and pulled a purple and black neck tag from the security booth inside the door. He handed it to me.

"Am I off limits", I asked, feeling some kind of way. Purple and black tags meant that anyone could talk or mingle with me, but that no one could approach me for a scene or make a request.

"Mistress Lila requests you wear it until you acclimate to being here again", he told me. "When you are ready just turn it in to any of the security staff. She told me specifically that she wanted you to feel as comfortable as possible while here. We have your favorite table reserved if you want it, as well as beverages you like and snacks just for you. I helped with those myself. I made sure the music tonight was a lot of your favorites from metal to techno. I am to follow you tonight and serve in place of a normal submissive for you.

No obligations, this is only the respect Mistress Lila wants to show you."

"That's a lot of extra effort for an outcast", I said.

"You are not an outcast", he almost shouted. He got himself under control quickly. "You founded this place. You built it. You stood up to the gangs and the cops to keep us free to live our lives. You are home", he said. We had walked into the main room of the dungeon, or club if it made you feel better, and people turned to stare at us. Many of them waved or smiled as they recognized me. A few whispered or stared, but the signs of recognition and acceptance were immediate. And very gratifying to a guy who had cut himself off from everything.

"Sir, please", Elias said and pointed to the bar. It was a unique place with a large sign over the center reading "Fire and Ice". The concept was simple and elegant. One half was made of wood and anything that represented fire. SImulated charcoal braziers and a long faux fireplace decorated the wooden bar itself. That half served hot food. The second half was an ice theme and made of crystal and glass and served all kinds of drinks, none of which were alcoholic. Alcohol and drugs were forbidden in Heller. There was a main stage for demonstrations, teaching circles, and public scenes that was open once the bar closed for breaks. It was the most amazingly overdone concessions area, but damn if it wasn't beautiful. Couches lined many of the walls as well as a few places in the floor not open for wrestling, rigging, or scenes. Several tables sat just to the side of the bar on a small raised platform. I followed his direction and went to the bar.

The main floor was maybe half full of people. There was a rigging scene going on over to the side, a woman being tied with a beautiful Shibari technique. In another area a man was being flogged by two other men and seemed to be having a great time. Several other mini scenes were happening throughout the throng. A boot black had set up her stand near the stage and was waiting for clients.

"One ice water coming up", the girl behind the bar said. She had red and blue hair and was wearing sparkly shorts and suspenders with no top. Her suspenders barely covered her nipples but managed to hold back her firm breasts.

"Emma", I asked.

"It's good to see you Cy", she said with an appraising glance. "You're looking good. Rough, but good", she said and winked at me.

"And you're still a good liar. It's really good to see you girl", I said with the first genuine smile I'd had all day. She passed over a half frozen bottle of water, still sealed, from behind the bar.

"It's sealed and exactly the way you like it", she said and grinned. "Do you need anything else?"

"Old habits die hard", I told her, referring to the water. "No, I shouldn't need anything else, but thank you", I said. I had started to turn away.

"Hey, can I say something", she asked. I turned back to her.

"When have you ever not spoken your mind", I asked.

"Follow Elias's lead tonight. Mistress Lila has really looked out for him and Mistress Kalya. Hell, for all of us. Please just let him do what he's supposed to tonight."

"Is there trouble", I asked.

"Not like you mean Cy", she said. "It's more that Mistress Lila has made this a point of honor for all of Heller and Elias and Kalya have staked their entire house reputation on being the ones to perform this service. Word is Kalya herself would have subbed for you tonight but everyone thought a male would be better. So please, just let him do it". She seemed almost like she was pleading.

"In other words don't be a stubborn ass and go with the flow", I said.

"Something like that", she shot back. I nodded to her. Someone had made this a very big deal. I'd bite, at least for a while.

"Elias", I said.

"Yes, sir", he asked.

"Please show me to my table and then let Mistress Lila know I'm here", I told him. He smiled a big goofy smile and led me to the table near the wall with the best view of the room. A little placard sat on the table reading, "Reserved for C. Magnus". I sat down and thanked Elias. I leaned back in the chair and sipped my water. The floor was abuzz with people talking, laughing, and all sorts of kinks being played out. The entire room was alive. Old school techno rang out across the floor but wasn't so loud you couldn't have a conversation. Or hear the moans or gasps from the members for that matter. I sat and watched and just vibed to the scene. Security kept an eye on me but it was more to keep away the curious than because it was me. A few people wandered over to catch up for a few minutes here or there but I could tell word had gone out to give me space. After maybe fifteen minutes Elias popped back up at my elbow.

"Mistress Lila wants to know if you will join her upstairs or if she should come to you", he asked.

"Let's join her upstairs", I said and stood. Elias led me down one of the hallways filled with different rooms. Many of the rooms had different purposes. Massage, medical play, pure bondage, a latex room, a small section for puppy play etc. At the end of the hall was a large play cross next to a stairway. A blond female was strapped to the cross with her back exposed as her Dom or Domme, I couldn't tell from the angle, worked her ass over with a dragon tail. It would have been fun to watch but I was on business. Elias led us up the wide staircase to the second floor office.

It was a large room with one entire wall of windows staring out into the night. Red, purple, and black bolts of fabric hung from the ceiling creating the illusion of partitions throughout the open space. A beautiful oak desk sat near a fireplace and the old wooden floor was covered in rugs of every color and hue. Lila half sat on the edge of the desk waiting for me.

"Thank you for joining me", she said.

"You went to a lot of effort to have me hear", I said to her.

"This was yours long before it was mine", she said.

"It's a good place. A safe place for many", I said.

"And it will be for as long as you wish it to be, you have my word", she said and glanced at Elias.

"I apologize Elias, would you please wait for me at the bottom of the stairs", I asked him. "I'm not sure how long I will be up here, but if it's more than about twenty minutes just go enjoy yourself and I'll send for you."

"Absolutely", he said and left the room.

"So, why did you want me to come here", I asked her.

"I thought it would be a more comfortable place for you to meet me", she said.

"Familiar maybe, not sure about comfortable", I told her.

"Your exile is your choice, not the choice of the people here", she said.

"Yeah, I know", I said. "So, what did you want to talk about?"

"I want you to help me kill Marcus", she said. She was dead serious. He he, dead serious.

"No", I said simply.

"No", she asked.

"No", I said again.

"And may I ask why not", she asked.

"Because I'm going to kill the motherfucker myself", I said. It was a flat unemotional statement. A statement of utter fact.

"And you think you can do this yourself", she asked. She shifted to sit completely on the desk, her feet barely dangling off the floor.

"Yep", I said.

"I didn't take you for a fool", she said.

"Lady, you don't know me, you sure don't know what I can do", I told her.

"Where is your dog", she suddenly asked. I opened my leather jacket on one side so she could see the puppy snoozing against my chest.

"Ah", she said with a smile. Then she got back on track. "Do you know what I am", she asked.

"Another hunter", I asked, but I made sure I sounded uninterested.

"Ha", she said. "I was the lawgiver of my plane. Once I was Princess of the Land of Shadow and Night. I battled for two hundred of your years to keep the balance between your plane and mine. Marcus shattered that balance. In his quest to control the nihil, he shattered our dimension. All of my people were lost. It was the shade of a hunter named Isabelle who guided me here. Your grandmother Isabelle who brought me forth to help avenge her. And I will avenge her. She and the shades of my world demand Marcus's blood, his very soul, shall writhe under my blade", she said all this with a vehemence I felt in my soul.

"And how long have you been here", I asked.

"Four human years", she said.

"And he's still alive", I asked.

"Marcus is like smoke. He blows in the wind, weaves through each trap. It is very frustrating", she said and blew a lock of her hair out of her face.

"So why not use me as bait", I asked.

"Bait", she queried.

"Marcus keeps following me, yanking my chain. Tail me until he shows up and I'll lead him to a good place. Then I'll kill him. If he kills me instead, you have your shot", I said coldly.

"And why not work together", she asked.

"Because I owe Marcus and this is my plane", I told her with as much rage as she had shown to me.

"No", she said.

"No", I demanded.

"No", she said. "I will not play a part in your death, and this is a plan made to see you dead."

"Then stand back and I'll handle it myself", I told her and started to leave.

"Cy, wait", she said softly. "Please, let me help you. Please", she said again.

"Why", I asked.

"Because it was the last wish of your Grandmother Isabelle. Her only request for the favor of saving my life", she said.

"Well... FUCK", I said. She smiled a little. She knew she had me.

Chapter Fifteen

"So what now", I asked. Lila looked at me for a minute then slid her shirt over her head. She stood in elegant black pants and a beautiful black lacy bra. She was a contrast of moon faded skin and dark shadows. Her ebon hair glided over one shoulder to drape above her breast and she looked at me knowingly.

"Take off that black and purple tag and I'll give you a few ideas", she said.

"This tag", I asked and held it out.

"Yes, that one", she replied and peeled her pants off, teasing me slowly. She stood waiting in her black bra and panties. In that moment I wasn't sure if she was a blessing or a curse. She could have been cure or poison, but either way I was going to taste her. I gently removed the tag from my neck and placed it on a table. Feeling a rumble in my jacket I pulled the puppy from my jacket and set him on a chair nearby.

"Don't watch, you're too young", I muttered to him and he snorted and curled up into a ball. I turned back to Lila and peeled off my jacket slowly. Teasing her as she had teased me. She watched every movement as intensely as I had watched her. I knew without a doubt she was as hungry for me as I was for her.

"What are you waiting for", she asked and looked at me from the fall of her hair. I moved to her. I walked slowly, letting her feel the effect of me moving softly and intently towards her. I wanted her to feel the intensity of my approach in that stomach clenching way rough dangerous sex brought. Because we were both rough. We were both dangerous. And this would be both a thing of violence and beauty.

I stopped in front of her for a moment, almost touching and listened to her breath come faster. I reached out and grabbed her by her hair. Not to hurt, not yet at least, but to take control of her. She moaned and tilted her face up to me. I used my other hand to cup her jaw gently as I lowered my mouth to hers. She opened her mouth greedily and placed her hands on my chest pressing her body into me. I teased her lips with my tongue before gently entering her full mouth. She tasted like cinnamon and I lost a little of my hard won control as I kissed her more roughly, pushing my tongue deeper into her mouth and clenching her hair tighter. She responded, kissing me back and grinding her hips into my rock hard cock.

I slid my hands down the front of her body until I found her bra. My tongue still dancing with hers I gently lifted the cups and allowed her breasts to fall free as I pulled her bra over her head. I buried my face between her breasts and she giggled lightly as my beard tickled her breasts. She stopped giggling and gasped when I latched my mouth around her right nipple. I traced her nipple in circles with my tongue as I let her feel my teeth sink gently into her areola. She grabbed fistfuls of my hair and pulled my mouth tighter into her breast.

"Yes, hurt me, please", she gasped.

I bit gently at first but then harder as she cried out and begged for me. I slowly let go to the sound of her whimpers as I moved to her left nipple and repeated my actions. She tensed and screamed as I bit down but kept pulling me into her chest harder. I wanted to know if both sets of lips tasted equally delicious so I released her nipple and stood. I grabbed two handfuls of her amazing ass and lifted her onto the desk. I hooked a nearby office chair with my foot and pulled it close to me while I pushed her back onto the desk. I gently removed her panties as she looked up at me and writhed on the cold desk.

I sat on the chair and licked my way up her thighs. I could smell the delicious treat awaiting me and couldn't wait to feel her orgasm drip from my beard. Sitting at her center I gently traced her lower lips with my tongue just as I had her mouth. She whimpered again and started begging. I licked her crease slowly, loving the anticipation as much as the taste and feel of her. I slowly moved her folds apart so that I could bury my face between her legs. I lapped slowly and gently at the warm bud in her center. She arched and writhed as my tongue moved slowly in circles and across her. When I could sense she was close I stopped. I pulled back.

"Do not cum unless I tell you to", I told her.

"Oh please, yes please", she said but I wasn't sure she really understood what I was saying. I buried my face once again and began to lick more forcefully. Every time I felt her clench down I would stop, edging her mercilessly until she began to cry and scream.

"Please, fuck, please let me cum", she shouted. I continued to lick and stop until my entire face was covered with her nectar.

"Cum", I said to her and a scream graced my ears as her entire body convulsed with her orgasm. She lay shaking as I held still, gently flicking her bud with my tongue from time to time so I could hear her gasp. Slowly I began to lick and edge her again. She didn't last nearly as long this time before begging for release.

"Cum", I ordered again and her body repeated it's clench and shake which was the greatest thank you I knew she could express. I pulled back and stood, kicking the chair away from us. I grabbed her firmly by her hair and hand. I used her hand to pull her from the desk keeping just enough tension in her hair for her to feel but not enough that it would really hurt. I lowered her to her knees in front of me. She was still reeling from the last orgasm and the change in position as I unfastened my belt and pulled it from my pants. I set it on the desk, we might need it later. I opened my pants letting my erection free from the tight jeans.

Before I could say anything she had opened her mouth and swallowed the length of me. My girth gave her some trouble as I was almost as big around as I was long but she was determined to swallow all of me. Her warm wet mouth felt so amazing along my hardness and my head flew back as my back arched. She used my body's momentum to thrust my cock further into her mouth and held me there. She let me enjoy the sensation before using her tongue and mouth to explore every inch of my erection. I knew if I didn't stop her soon I'd disappoint both of us but she felt so amazing I had to force myself to drag her off my cock. I grabbed her hair and firmly pulled her to her feet. A small string of saliva clung from her lower lip to the head of my cock and I almost lost control at the sight. I turned her back around and bent her over the desk. I pulled my belt from the desk and showed it to her.

"Oh fuck yes please", she begged and writhed.

I wrapped the belt around my hand and then swung it, making a delicious sound as it struck her ass cheek. The flesh of her ass moved with the impact and was hypnotizing as she cried out from the impact. I swung again and again, slowly increasing the strength of the swings so that her body warmed to the sensation of the pain. She cried out with each strike, quivering with it. Her body begged for more as her mouth shrieked her pleasure in the pain. Red stripes criss crossed the flesh of her ass as I methodically struck every inch of her delicious ass with the aged leather. Her excitement fueled my own and I didn't know if I had ever been more aroused than in this moment! When I couldn't take the build up anymore I tossed the belt onto the desk beside her.

I managed to finish removing my pants, shirt, and shoes in record time. I stood behind her, running my hands along her reddened ass admiringly. The tip of my cock brushed against her folds as I touched her, making her arch and whimper. She moaned and gasped with each touch but I knew she would have let me do a lot more had I wanted to.

I wrapped my hand around my cock and used the other to open her folds.

"Yes, fuck me, please, fuck me", she begged.

I gently pushed myself against her tightness. I had to be careful not to thrust into her until her body relaxed and accepted me. But slowly I pushed inside as she whimpered and arched against the desk. She lifted her upper body just enough for me to see her beautiful breasts pooled under her body as I pushed the last of myself inside of her. I could feel my control slipping in the first few thrusts.

"Don't cum until I tell you", I reminded her. She was too drunk on the scene to reply coherently. I grabbed both hips and began thrusting into her. Her striped ass moved beautifully in recoil with each thrust deeper and deeper. She clenched around my cock and I knew neither of us was going to last much longer.

"Cum", I commanded and she shrieked. Her entire body lifted off the desk with her orgasm as I spilled hot and fierce inside of her. We writhed together in that moment, joined in one continuous orgasm shared between two bodies. For a split second it felt like our souls slid along each other as we climaxed and shook together. I stood stunned and buried deep inside her body. Every jerk and spasm my body committed elicited gasps and moans from the beautiful woman under me. Neither of us could move. I'm not sure I could even remember what my body felt like. Slowly I managed to draw out of her and she cried out again, another orgasm rocking her from my departure. I stood lost and gasping as I tried to help her up, but neither of us could make our bodies move. Finally I found the chair I had been sitting in earlier and collapsed into it. The room was silent except for our heavy breathing. After several moments she managed to climb off the desk and stagger the couple of feet to me. She dropped to her knees and looked up at me.

"I grace your beard so it's only fair the taste of us fills my mouth", she said and then took my still hard cock into her mouth. I gasped and my spine arched as she licked every inch of me clean. I could tell she was enjoying it by how thorough she was in running her lips and tongue over every inch of me. She took her time before finishing and laying her head on my thigh. We sat naked in the large room, silent and blissful in the aftermath of mind blowing sex.

"So, food or nap", I asked her and she started laughing. She had a beautiful laugh too.

Chapter Sixteen

We basked in the afterglow until we both suddenly realized we were cold. Lila had a king size bed against the far wall under the windows. We helped each other stumble to the bed and wrapped ourselves in the fur blankets. I laughed softly.

"What's funny", she asked.

"I used to have one of these faux fur blankets on my bed. I loved it", I told her.

"Except that this is real fur", she mumbled to me, still flying from the scene and sex. I thought about that for a bit as her breathing evened into sleep. I lay on my back, a beautiful woman nestled against me, and thought about the last few days.

The perspective change was a real bitch but I hadn't started drooling and beating my head into a wall, so I felt like I'd accomplished something at least. My grandmother's secret life bothered me. How had I not known? Hell, had dad known and just never said anything? There were still a lot of pieces to fit to the puzzle, but one thing was sure. Marcus needed to be brought to justice. Unfortunately, human justice wasn't built for this. Which meant this would have to be an off the books job. I'd done those for Uncle

Sugar. It's one of the many reasons why I left. But this time I was doing it knowing this was someone who had to be stopped. I'd learned that some folks just couldn't be fixed. There was no rehabilitation for a certain kind of evil. I fell asleep beside Lila and for once, I didn't have nightmares.

Lila and I were jarred awake by a drooling thirty pound ball of fur and terror jumping onto our chests and mauling us with puppy breath. Lila groaned and yanked the blankets over her head, uncovering me in the process.

"What the hell", I mumbled. My tiny puppy was now a mid-sized puppy. How? How long did we sleep? "Lila, what happened to my dog", I asked her.

"He's a hellhound Cy", she mumbled. "He's going to grow quickly at first so that he's ready for when you need him".

"Huh", I said. The dog started dragging the blanket off of me and growling.

"Your dog, your problem", Lila said and burrowed into the bed.

"Thanks, you're all heart", I told her and started to get up. The dog brought me one of my boots like that was all I needed and started pacing to the door. I managed to stumble into my pants and pull my shirt over my head. We went down the back steps to the private owner's entrance. I opened the door and the dog sprinted out into the light. And there sat Clara's unmarked SUV. In the rear parking area. And I was half dressed and still barefoot. Well, shit!

The driver's side window rolled down and a cup of coffee was dangled out of the window. Ah, fuck it, I was caught. Might as well give up gracefully. I shoved my feet into my boots, thanked the combat gods for bungee shoe laces, and walked over. Clara wolf whistled at me as I approached. I had forgotten my coat. Dog suddenly stopped, looked at me, and sprinted back through the open door. I stood looking at Clara confused until a moment later, the half grown pup came back out the door dragging my coat and mostly getting tangled up in it. I rescued him and my leather and petted him to thank him. He licked me and ran back out to attack the wind and just be a puppy.

"When did you get a dog", Clara asked.

"It's been very recent. Are you following me", I asked.

"Yep", she said and sipped. I took the coffee from her gingerly and took my own sip. She was playing it really cool, which meant she was trying to get to me somehow.

"Do I ask how or why", I wondered aloud.

"Good question", she said. She was looking way too pleased with herself.

"Cy". a voice called from the second floor window. We both looked up. Lila had poked her upper body out the upstairs window. She was sleep tousled and dressed only in the fur comforter. "Bring her up here and let's have breakfast. I'm hungry and there's a lot to talk about", Lila said. At the mention of the word breakfast the dog barked and charged back upstairs.

"Ever been in a BDSM Dungeon before", I asked Clara.

"No", she said and blushed furiously.

"Then please come in", I said and laughed. She blushed harder. But she turned off the SUV and started inside. Major brownie points for her, she didn't hesitate. Maybe she wasn't as vanilla as I thought.

"You ok going in here", I asked when we got to the door.

"Afraid your girlfriend will be uncomfortable", she asked, ribbing me gently.

"More afraid I'll turn you to the dark side", I said.

"If anybody could", she mumbled and headed inside. I stood there for a minute wondering if I had heard what I thought I had heard. I shrugged and followed her upstairs. About halfway up I stopped her again.

"Hey, look, you don't have to do this", I told her. "I can see where this might be a little sticky", I said.

"Sticky", she asked with a smirk.

"Fine fine", I said.

"It's ok Cy, I'm a big girl. This doesn't wig me out", she told me.

I followed Clara into the office which I guess was now also an apartment to find Lila scrambling eggs on a small stove and Clara sitting in one of the overstuffed chairs. Lila had thrown on tights and a t- shirt but that was obviously about all. The dog was sitting patiently near the stove and Lila was throwing him the occasional scrap. Lila was in her element but Clara was obviously not. This was getting to her quick.

"Clara Fields, this is Lila", I said. "Lila meet Clara", I finished. Lame I know but what else was I supposed to say?

"Welcome Clara", Lila said over her shoulder. "Do you want breakfast", she asked.

"I brought some", Clara said and held up her coffee. "But thank you", she said.

"Of course", Lila said and continued cooking. "I feel I need to apologize to you", Lila continued.

"To me", Clara asked in confusion.

"I did not know you and Cy were a thing. I try never to poach", Lila said and gave me a glare.

"Wha-", Clara sputtered and spit coffee all over herself. Lila tossed her a clean dishrag and Clara began blotting herself. "Cy's not mine", Clara said.

"Oh good", Lila said. "The emotions coming off of you suggested that you two were an item".

"Well we're not", Clara denied but wouldn't look at either of us.

"Why not", Lila asked.

"Why not what", Clara said.

"Do you not want him", Lila asked Clara but looked at me.

"Wait", Clara interrupted. "You can sense my emotions", she asked.

"Among other things, yes", Lila answered. "It's a special gift. But let's not change the subject, do you not want him", Lila asked again.

"Look, whatever I feel towards Cy is kinda my business", Clara explained. "I'm not trying to be ugly but I don't know you so please leave my emotions to me".

"As you wish, I didn't mean any offense", Lila said as she scraped two large portions of eggs on two plates and a smaller portion onto a third. I looked at them both confused.

"Can someone clue me in please", I asked, looking from one to the other.

"My people did not hold back their love from each other. This monogamish fantasy you cling to in this world would be unheard of in mine. I have no problem with you having other partners, Cy. Though I believe you and I started something last night, a bond really, I will never ask you to hold yourself back from exploring and experiencing real love", Lila told me. "Not sex or cheap thrills, these I will not abide. But love, love is different", she told both of us. She put the plate with the smaller portion on the floor for the dog and he willingly enjoyed his noms. I wasn't so happy. Lila looked first at me standing there confused and then at Clara sunk deep into her chair. Lila went to Clara and gave her the most amazing smile. Lila held her hand out to Clara and Clara took it. Lila drew Clara to her feet and then slowly over to me.

"I did not mean to stir something that I did not understand, but know that among my people this is not forbidden. Whatever you two choose to do about it, ignore it or explore it, just understand that I am ok either way", Lila said. Her eyes were so kind. I took Clara's chin in my hand and gently pulled her to look at me.

"Clara, I like you, I really do, but you know I've never been that guy", I told her. Told them both really.

"I know, Cy", she said. "I don't want to screw up an amazing friendship. You've taught me so much, helped me, and been a real friend. I don't want to lose that".

I couldn't let the pain in her eyes continue but I wasn't the kind of guy who could just sleep with one woman and then another. I hugged her to me tightly and pressed her head under my chin and she sobbed a little. I didn't know if she was crying because I wouldn't or relieved that I hadn't. I looked at Lila. She wasn't just smiling, she was beaming and holding her clasped hands under her chin.

"Let us eat", she said. "And after, if you two wish some privacy to talk, my home is yours".

"Thank you", Clara said.

"That's very kind of you, but I think this is going to take a while to figure out", I said.

"Um…", Clara said and pulled slightly away from me.

"I agree with Cy, we may never figure this out", Clara said. I tried to push past my obvious confusion and focus on something more stable. Business, focus on business.

"So how did you find me", I asked Clara as I sat on the floor to eat. The dog came over and sat next to me, obviously trying to figure out how to get my food without me noticing.

"Do you remember George from forensics", she asked.

"Yeah, really into computers, loves anime, good attention to detail on a case", I said.

"Yeah, so about a month after you left Sam and I bribed him with a light novel series to hack your phone settings and give us access to your phone finder app", she said with a grin.

"You bugged my phone", I asked.

"No, we tracked your phone. And do not ask what we had to do to get those books. You wouldn't believe how hard that was", she said with a shudder.

"So you both watch me", I asked. I would have been offended but I was just impressed. The dirty tricks department was usually my bag and they were the law and order crew. Guess I had rubbed off on them.

"Not generally, but when those government issued clones started showing up, Sam asked me to keep an eye on you", she said.

"There are clones", Lila piped in.

"No", Clara said and laughed. "These guys say they're Feds of some kind. But they look alike, dress alike, and talk the same so they might as well be".

"I will inquire about this", Lila said to me. "We have fallen afoul of human governments before. If they are poking around this may be a bigger problem".

"Well, one problem at a time", I told her.

"So, why were you waiting for me this morning", I asked Clara.

"When Sam saw where your pin had been most of the night he asked me to come check on you. He said that being here all night would either mean you were finally coming out of your fugue or you had slipped a gear really badly". I wanted to argue but it was accurate.

"And did you know what this place was", I asked.

"Sam told me", she said and looked down, blushing again.

"It took guts for you to come sit a stake out then. Thank you", I told her. She looked up and beamed at me. It was a smile I would have moved worlds for.

"So, has Cy told you anything about the last few days", Lila asked Clara.

"Some", she said, "but at the time it was very vague".

"He has not had much time to assimilate to a lifetime of experience", Lila said. "I was hoping you would step forward to help him"

"I'd love to, but I don't know how", Clara said.

"Absolutely not", I interrupted. "I am not dragging her into this. I won't see her killed for this."

"It's not your choice, Cy", Clara told me. She was hot, like raging mad.

"I agree with her Cy", Lila said. "Marcus cannot be stopped without help". We sat in silence for a minute and then the dog sat up on alert. He looked around, then went and grabbed my phone off the floor. He trotted up to me and dropped it on my lap. It rang and Clara looked from me to the dog. Lila immediately rose and and went to an armoire against one wall. I wiped the drool off the phone and looked at the Caller I.D. It read Betty Clark. I answered the phone in time to see Lila open the armoire which was filled with weapons.

Hello", I said goggling at Lila, whose back was to me.

"Cy, Nina's missing", Betty said.

Chapter Seventeen

"What do you mean missing", I asked.

"She didn't come home last night", Betty said.

"Ok, that's not necessarily the end of the world", I said, "she's seventeen."

"Cy, I searched her room when she still wasn't home this morning. I found some of the same books Marcus used back when I was young", she said. "Cy, what if Marcus has her?"

"Have you told Sam yet", I asked.

"No, you know what happens if I tell him", she said.

"Yeah, I do", I said, but I was focused on the amount of sheer hardware Lila was pulling out of the armoire. Clara had gotten the clue and had her notebook.

"Betty, I'm putting you on speakerphone. Clara and a friend of mine named Lila are with me", I told her.

"Oh, thank god Clara's there", Betty's voice strained from the phone's speaker. Clara was in full cop mode.

"What's the last ping on Nina's phone", I asked.

"The pin is showing at a house on old 311 near 74", she told me.

"Across from an old factory about a quarter mile from 74", I asked. I had a bad feeling.

"Yes, it last updated six minutes ago", Betty said.

"Send access to the account to Clara please", I told her.

"I will", she said. "Cy, find my baby before I have to tell Sam", she said.

"I'm on it", I said. We hung up. Lila tossed me a vest and a tactical shotgun. She looked at Clara.

"Do you have a tactical load out", Lila asked.

"In the SUV", Clara confirmed. "Why doesn't Betty want you to tell Sam", Clara asked me.

"You didn't know Sam back in the day. He got real violent real quick when it was justified. We've always been afraid for Sam if his family was ever threatened. I'm cold and methodical, he's more of a nuke the continent kind of guy", I told her.

"Sam", she asked in shock.

"The one and only", I told her as I buttoned up.

"You know this is a trap right", Lila asked us. I nodded. It was pretty obvious. Clara nodded as well.

"Whose car are we taking", Clara asked.

"Yours", I said. Lila looked a question at me.

"Cy, I can't run blue lights without a reason", she said. "Dispatch will see it".

"The hell you can't" I said and started heading downstairs. I got back on my phone and called in a chit. The phone rang twice.

"If you're calling me hell has broken through in Forsyth County", the gruff voice said.

"Sam's daughter has been kidnapped. I'm with Clara. We will be running a silent code 1. I need you to keep it off the books Major", I said.

"Fuck, does Sam know", my former SWAT Commander asked.

"Not yet and we're trying to get to Nina first", I said.

"I should have known, there hasn't been anything on Channel One about bodies on the ground. Ok, what area, I'll pull the units in that Zone", he said. I told him.

"Go, do what you need to, bring her home safe", he said. "I'll do what I can with the aftermath", and with that he hung up. The four of us, dog included, piled into the SUV and Clara did her best to burn the tires off the SUV the whole way there. We shut off the sirens two miles out and got off the exit, turning left. I had Clara stop about five hundred yards from the pin on her phone. The place wasn't a house. It was an abandoned retirement home. It was a large dilapidated complex. The grass was really high which was good for us if we wanted a stealth approach, but bad because we didn't really have time. But if we rushed in we could get dead quick. Dead didn't help Nina.

"How do you want to do this", Clara asked.

"I'll recon first, then report back", I told her.

"No", Lila said.

"Why not", I asked.

"Because if it's a trap he'll be looking for you. And we have someone who can do the recon and never be seen", she said and looked at my dog. I looked at him.

"Can you do that", I asked him. He gave a gentle bark and leapt out the open window.

"Cy, I need you to trust me. I want you to lean your head back and think only of your dog. The feel of his fur, his scent", Lila said.

"What", I asked.

"Do it now", she commanded. I shut up and did it. After a few breaths I could feel paws on the earth and smell wood rot and pollen. I snapped back up.

"What the fuck", I said.

"You're seeing through his eyes. Now focus", Lila said.

"What am I, the fucking Beastmaster", I asked and closed my eyes again. My dog was laying in the weeds waiting. I guessed he was waiting for me. I watched as he moved carefully around the complex, looking and smelling for disturbances on the ground. He tracked similar to one of our Police K9's, gotta love the violent bastards, so I understood exactly what he was doing. As he circled around behind the complex I could smell something strange. It smelled like a really old dead body. An image of Marcus flashed in my mind. Was my dog trying to tell me this smell was Marcus? The image flashed again. Yep, message received. The dog tracked closer to what had probably once been the chapel. I smelled something sweet and the undertone of blood. I wanted to panic but somehow I knew this was normal. The smell was a human female and the blood smell was... ahem... well her business and not mine. The dog got closer and I could hear Marcus talking to someone.

"Don't worry, Cy will be here soon. And when he comes I'll let you go", he soothed. If the voice of a maniac could be soothing.

"Fuck you, untie me and I'll kill you my fucking self you son of a bitch", Nina's voice said. That's my girl I thought proudly. Stupid and angry, I knew she had to be mine after all! I thought hard at my dog to look for doors or windows.

He was way ahead of me. He deliberately looked at a path along the side of the building we could approach from, and then showed me a rotten door with windows a good four feet away on either side. Good, we could breach and clear. I thought very hard for him to come back and I could feel him moving in my direction as I came out of it. I came back in a rush.

"Ooof, that sucks", I said, gasping for air and trying not to vomit. I would not puke, I would not, I refused. The spinning slowly settled down and my stomach stopped trying to climb through my belly button.

"Take a moment, the first few times can be difficult", Lila said.

"Ugh, yeah, difficult is a word for it", I said.

"Suck it up Cy", Clara said. Yep, sympathy was definitely somewhere between shit and syphilis in today's dictionary. "What did you find", she asked.

"Looks like Marcus and Nina are the only two in there. Nina's alive and cussing. Dog has us a path. We're going to breach at the rear of what looks like an old chapel. One wooden rotted door, three hinges, standard door knob, no deadbolt. A window on each side of the door, about three to four feet to either side", I told them.

"Do you have breaching rounds", Clara asked.

"No, it looks like standard load, one slug and then buckshot. Any in here", I asked.

"No, but I have two 'bangs", she said.

"You have flashbangs", I asked.

"Times are tough all over Cy", she said with a grin.

"Won't the flashbangs hurt the girl", Lila asked.

"Shit, yeah we can't use them. They won't hurt her as long as they don't land close but there's a huge risk of fire", I said.

"Then allow me to take care of the door", Lila said and exited the vehicle. We followed and met the dog at the fenceline to the nursing home. He turned and led us through the grass and along the path around back. I took point watching for booby traps and Clara had the rear. We moved slow but well. Slow is smooth and smooth is fast. We got around back and heard Nina yelling.

"Get away from me you son of a bitch", Nina screamed. Lila's head jerked up and her eyes burned with a purple fire. We were almost at the door.

"No", Nina screamed and Lila lost it. Purple fire surrounded both of her hands and she punched them both into the wall. There was a horrendous sound and a four foot by five foot section of wall disintegrated in her hands. Fuck it, we'd do it live. I leapt through the hole and landed on my side, shotgun up. Marcus was pantsless and bending over Nina who was tied up on the floor. I fired. I emptied the shotgun into the son of a bitch's chest. Six rounds dead center at about eight feet. There wasn't a whole lot of center mass left when I ran empty. Lila jumped over me, twin blades in her hands. Something attacked her as soon as she entered. It was as black as the shadows in the chapel and all I could see was teeth and claws and a huge mouth.

"Get the girl", Lila shouted as her blades flashed a silver purple pattern in the air.

"Clara, help Lila", I shouted but I doubted she could hear me. None of us were wearing ear plugs and gunshots in confined places were about like sticking your head in a speaker at a death metal concert. I started to run to Lila but my dog was already there. He was in his large scary apocalypse bringing form. He was standing over Nina smelling her. Once he was apparently happy with what he smelled he carefully bit through the steel cuffs on Nina's wrists and ankles. She clung to the ferocious beast as we fought. I was reloading the shotgun three rounds at a time when Clara came through the opening and was knocked flat by another of the quadrupeds from Freddy Kreugars fan club. Clara screamed.

"Fuck this", I yelled and reached deep inside. I snapped the shotgun up and blue fire gleamed from the breach. I fired two rounds into the head of Clara's attacker and it exploded. One round left! I spun and Lila tossed her beast against the wall. I fired as it impacted and it too detonated. I dropped the shotgun and transitioned to my side arm and scanned. Deep breaths, control the adrenaline. I didn't see any other threats. Clara rushed to Nina and the dog let her pass. A booming laugh echoed through the chapel. It was Marcus. But how, I had blown holes right through him.

"I will see you soon Cy", his voice echoed through the chapel.

"FUCK", I screamed. We stood panting and Clara was comforting Nina in the corner. Lila gave me a thumbs up so I went over to them. Nina saw me.

"Uncle Cy", she yelled and jumped into my arms. She was balling. Hell, I might've balled too. She clung to me and cried. I couldn't do anything but hold her back and keep telling her it was ok. As sound returned we could hear sirens slowly approaching. Well, it had been ok. Could I get lucky enough for Sam to not be the first on scene? I took my coat off and covered Nina with it. I didn't want Sam to see her ripped blouse. I couldn't stop him from seeing her bloody lip and black eye, but I could do this. I did it for both of their sakes.

Chapter Eighteen

We made our way back out front as the patrol cars rolled up. Clara walked out in front, holding her badge high. It was the best option for us to not get shot by the responding cops. Luckily there wouldn't be any bodies to link to us and Nina balled up in my arms and crying would cut us some slack. How had Marcus gotten up and walked away from that? I knew I'd seen holes blown all the way through his chest. Hell most of his chest had been completely gone.

I was carrying Nina in my arms like some romance novel as the cop cars skidded to a stop in front of us. The deputies sprung out of their cars then paused. I guess they weren't expecting this site to be what they found on arrival.

"We need EMS for an assault victim", Clara shouted at the deputies. One of them immediately keyed up on their radio to have EMS respond to the scene.

"How many injured", the deputy called out.

"One female", Clara called back. It was procedure. Better to have EMS come out and assess Nina instead of waiting. Nina burrowed tighter into my chest. A command staff car skidded to a halt behind the deputies and Major Murphy got out.

"Cy, Sam's thirty seconds behind me", he yelled in warning. I looked down at the girl cradled in my arms.

"Your dad's here", I said.

"He's going to totally freak", she said.

"Yep", I agreed and braced for the storm. Right about then Sam's SUV drifted into the gravel in front of the deputies cars. The acrid smell of burning brake pads told me how hard he had pushed the vehicle. He jumped out bristling with magazines, his main side arm, his back up, and a wicked AR clenched in his huge fist. Man wasn't playing.

"Nina", he screamed and sprinted to us.

"I'm ok", she tried to say but Sam wasn't hearing it. He snatched her out of my arms, clenching her tight and crying as he sank to his knees holding her. Clara came up and hugged me on one side and Lila did the same on the other. Major Murphy walked over to us.

"Good job, all three of you", he said. "How many perps", he asked.

"None that we saw", I said.

"Cy", Murphy said and approached me, "don't let me get burned on this".

"Major, I've never left you swinging. We located Nina in the back of this place. We only entered through one door and stayed in one room so as not to mess up any forensics. There were some wild dogs inside so you'll find a couple of shell casings because they were going to attack Nina. If there's anything else in there, we don't know about it", I told him.

"Will Clara write it that way", he asked.

"Clara will write the report any way you want", I told him.

"She's the pinnacle of an honest officer", he said doubtfully.

"This time's different", I said. "My team will support the report as needed". I realized too late what I said. Damn, old habits.

"For it to be your team, you'd have to come back asshole", he growled about an inch from my nose. His face was getting purple. "So, when you drag your sorry ass back into my office and retake your fucking oath, which is in my top drawer, they are your team again Captain, but until then you do not have the right to say that", he snarled. "Now I would dearly love to force you to pull your head out of your ass and drag you back to work, but HR says I can't do that. So, get your shit wired and be in my office soon, Cy. With promotion and pay. The Sheriff has a special assignment for you. Come see him". And with that he began to stalk off. He stopped and looked back at me. "Most people never get a second chance Cy", he said. I looked around. Clara and Sam were both staring open mouthed. Clara mouthed the word captain at me in shock. I didn't know what to think.

"You look sexy in that color purple Major", I called. He flipped me off without turning around and the deputies laughed. Sam stood up and tucked Nina under his arm. I was ready for him to deck me or yell at me or cuss me out. He walked over to me and I gently pushed Lila and Clara behind me. I wouldn't fight back. He reached out lightning quick with the arm not holding Nina and drug me to him. The giant muscular bastard all but snatched me off my feet. He held me so close that it took me a minute to realize he was hugging me and crying.

"Thank you Cy, thank you", he kept saying. I just stood there and held him while Clara gently extricated Nina from us. Clara took Nina over to the EMS unit that had just arrived and I held Sam and let him cry. All that emotion had to go somewhere and this was the best outcome I could imagine.

We stood by as Clara wove a great fiction about how we had located Nina and what we had found. The EMT's told us Nina had some bumps and scrapes but was otherwise unharmed. Sam rode with her to the hospital just to be sure. We all worked to keep Lila from being identified or having to give a statement. The deputies did a search of the area and finally Major Murphy determined that the property had been seized by the county and they wouldn't need a warrant to search the rest of the premises. The Major led the search.

After about five minutes we heard yelling from inside. I watched as the plywood covering one of the windows was smashed outward and one of the deputies stood vomiting. Dog gave a low growl and came to stand in front of me. Then the smell came. Rotting bodies. I can't describe the smell to you. You either know or you don't. If you do I'm sorry, if you don't just be happy with that. I heard a bellow from inside.

"Cy", Murphy called. "I need you". We all sprinted to the window. I could just see inside. Maybe fifteen bodies lay mutilated in the room. Body parts were severed, some pieces had been carved like they were being examined. One corpse had a huge bite taken out of the upper chest. Strange glyphs had been painted on the walls in blood and what looked like feces. It was too cold for flies thank goodness, but the smell was awful even in the cold.

"Who's down", I yelled.

"Help Johnson and Imenez out the window. I don't need them puking in here and contaminating the scene", he yelled. I shut up and extracted both deputies through the window. Lila came up to the window and looked inside. She blanched.

"Cy", she called. I went over to her. "These symbols, they're used only when one wants to summon multiple nihils at once", she whispered.

"Why would he want to do that", I asked.

"To build an army, or to collapse all the dimensions into one", she whispered back. That did not sound like a good thing. "He will be riding an immense power high. That may be why he survived today".

"We have to stop him", I said.

"Agreed", she said. I escorted both deputies back to their cars. I used Johnson's radio to call for more EMS, Detectives, and forensics. Funny how dispatch didn't ask me to identify myself. I asked Lila to stand with the deputies until I returned and went back to the window. Major Murphy stood hanging his head out the window and taking deep breaths.

"Cy, take your girlfriend and clear out. Clara can give you a ride back but then I'm going to need her back here. Backup is on the way and I can't have you found here", he said.

"You sure", I asked.

"I'm sure", he confirmed. "And Cy, make sure you get this bastard before you come back. I don't need that headache on the department", he said. I stared at him for a minute then cleared out. Lila and dog met me halfway back to the cars.

"Clara ran to get her vehicle", Lila said. Sure enough Clara pulled up a moment later and we all piled in.

"Where to", she asked.

"Anyone else hungry", I asked and Lila and Clara groaned. Dog just barked and wagged his tail. Maybe he'd like pup cups?

Chapter Nineteen

We ended up with burgers and I bought the dog his own double cheeseburger. I figured he'd earned it. I didn't think Clara was happy about the mess he made in the rear floorboard chomping down his burger, but he seemed happy. Clara dropped Lila and I back at Heller. She'd be busy for the next couple of days with reports and forensics so I knew she'd be too busy to get into much trouble. Lila and I figured a munch and nap was in order. We retired back to her office slash bedroom and did just that. I got up about an hour after dark and made use of Lila's shower. I wasn't sure if I was disappointed that Lila didn't get up and join me but I knew I wouldn't have said no. I got out and dressed only to find her still asleep in bed. I went over to her.

"Are you getting up", I asked.

"Uunnnhhhh", was her only reply. I gave up and found a pen and a writing pad on her desk. I wrote her a note telling her to call me when she got up and wrote my number down just in case. I thought about it for a minute and then wrote that I had enjoyed our time and that I'd like to see her again. I know, me and Prince Valiant, always risking the friend zone for being a nice guy. Besides, I had a hunch I wanted to try out anyway. I nodded at Dog, who looked like he had grown another hand or so, and we headed to my car.

If I could really control nihils I needed to test it. And if any one place would have one, or anything spooky for that matter, it was The Baxter House. If all this was real, I needed to get a handle on it and see the scope of where I was. Lack of intel could get you killed.

The Baxter house was a large abandoned two story house near Liberty St in Winston Salem. It grew up with the tobacco boom of the early and mid twentieth century. It was a rough neighborhood that kept a bad vibe. Locals thought it was because of rumors that the city had once paved roads over old graveyards that made up the dilapidated neighborhoods. Some local historians had tried to find out if the rumor was true but the answers all got hushed up about twenty years ago. No one had poked at it since. I figured a rough neighborhood after dark was about my speed tonight anyway. I called my manager at the pizza place to tell him I wouldn't be back for a while. He took it well and only cussed for about ten minutes. I let him vent, he was a good dude.

I pulled up in front of The Baxter House at about a quarter past ten. I'd seen the usual gang signs and a couple of prostitutes on the way in but nothing that really looked like trouble. The house looked ominous and still in the night. No one had lived there for years and most of the windows were boarded up. Old condemned notices had rotted from the door and I stepped careful, walking up what had once been a beautiful porch. Flecks of blue paint, what was known as Haint Blue here in North Carolina, still clung to the door. I froze for a moment, thinking I had seen movement in the only window not boarded up, but I didn't hear anything. I pulled out my pocket knife and quietly pried loose the couple of boards over the door. A little jiggling at the lock and the front door creaked open. And I mean creaked like the entrance to every nineteen seventies horror movie door ever! If I was a burglar my butt hole would be puckered so bad I'd turn inside out.

After a count of five I moved inside. Dog trotted behind me, sneezing at the dust and mold in the stagnant air. It didn't look like anyone had been inside for a very long time but there were a few hints of graffiti still clinging to the walls. We stood there for a minute, letting the silence fill the space. I kept getting flickers of movement around corners and at the edge of my vision. That overwhelming feeling of being watched filled my awareness and the hair on my body stood on end. I couldn't tell if it was hard to breathe because of the fear and adrenaline or from the mold. But like all intense encounters, I suddenly had to pee. It was a universal law of intense situations to always pee before you got into shit, or you'd have to for the entire fight. I didn't know why, but every person I'd ever met had the same problem.

I heard a shuffling from upstairs and Dog suddenly perked up. That let me know he'd heard it to. I walked through the living room to find an old staircase. Dog huffed at me and I looked down in time to see him start up the stairs first. He sniffed each step then gingerly put his weight on the old boards before moving forward. I stepped where he stepped figuring he understood the problem as well as I did. It took a minute but we made it to the second floor safely. We stood and listened and I thought I heard big band music coming from a room at the end of the hall. Strips of cloth wall paper hung in tatters over the lower paneling. There were a few rooms along the hall with the doors open and moonlight streamed through in patches to puddle on the ancient carpet. I had this mental vision of something lurking, waiting to grab me and drag me into one of the rooms. Inky black shadows sat clustered together in spots just large enough to make me think something could be lurking anywhere. My mind was so not my friend here.

The music seemed to be coming from a room at the end of the hall. The door was cracked a few inches and as I watched I thought I could see gentle light coming from the open space. My eyes had played tricks on me before in really dark places and I wasn't sure what was live and what was memorex. Knowing I needed to nut up or leave, I gathered my flagging bravery and started down the hallway. Every step sent up small puffs of dust and the floor creaked with each movement. If anyone was in there, they knew we were coming. As I drew closer to the door it became obvious that I really was seeing light coming from the room. Squatters, maybe? The music had grown louder but not loud enough to make out the tune. From inside I could hear a woman humming. I didn't know what else to do so I knocked. Yeah, I know that seems stupid, but hell, what else should I have done?

"Come in", a female voice called. Well, shit.

"I'm sorry to bother you", I started but was cut off.

"Oh, it's no bother", the female voice said. "Please come in". I pushed the door all the way open until it gently touched the wall. At least I knew no one would be hiding behind the door. It's the little things that will keep you alive. I carefully stepped in checking all the corners. Candles were placed in a couple of spots in the room. A small single bed sat in the corner. Near the window sat a desk with candles and a younger woman clothed in an early twentieth century dress with a high collar. Her dark hair was pinned up in a bun. Soft features gave her face warmth and life. On the table sat a stack of cards. Moonlight streamed through the window creating an eerie frame around the cards on the table.

"Are you here for a reading", she asked.

"A reading ma'am", I asked. This was too surreal.

"Of course, I've been waiting for you", she said. She sat in front of the cards and began shuffling.

"No ma'am, I didn't know that was an option. Honestly I came here just to try out a hunch", I told her.

"And what was your hypothesis, young man", she asked without looking at me.

"That this place was haunted", I said. Dog growled softly from within the doorway.

"Haunted, hhhmmmmm, mayhaps yes and mayhaps no", she said. "But I have lived here for longer than this house has stood. Do you know where this is", she asked.

"Winston Salem", I asked hopefully.

"Not quite", she said. "This is a house between worlds and I've been waiting for you Cy. Now come and sit".

"Why were you waiting for me", I asked. I sat in front of her, the moonlight playing from her hands as she laid out the cards.

"I was curious of course", she said.

"Curious about what", I asked. Two could play this game.

"Which path you'd choose", she said. "You do not yet know what you are, or where you fit in this game. But you still must choose how you will play".

"That's not very helpful", I told her.

"And who says I'm here to help you", she said. She had laid seven cards out on the table and began turning each one over. The art on the cards was horrific. Each showed a scene of horrible murder or torture. Ghastly images of pain and suffering.

"I live here so that I may read the fortunes of those who have come before and those who will go after", she said. "I see power and great truth in you Cy, but also the potential for great darkness. It is for you to choose which path you will follow."

"You sound a little like Loros", I said.

"He is another who chose his path. He is a shadow that I cannot read, but such is the way of the Shadow Kings", she said. Her words dripped ice down my spine. "Your path is here in the cards, but your choice remains clouded."

"Then why have me here", I asked.

"I wish to ask for your help", she said. "If you will, I will grant you a boon".

"What's the favor", I asked.

"Free the dead who reside here", she said. "Free them to move on for they have been trapped here too long. Come and see", she said and stood to look out the window. I joined her. Sixty, maybe seventy souls, stood at the rear of the house looking up at the window. They stood motionless, waiting as only the patient dead can wait.

"Just feel the land, and you will find what you seek", she said. I concentrated and there, near the skeleton of a child's swing set, I could feel a nihil. It was small but I could feel it. I willed it to open so that the dead could pass and I could see it shimmer to life. But this was unlike any nihil I had seen before. This one glowed with an amber light. It was like looking through a doorway into a world of peace. The dead turned as one and began filing through it. The woman clapped her hands beside me, almost breaking my concentration. One last man stopped and turned. He stared up at us for a moment before giving a little wave. Then he too was gone.

"Very well done", she said. I turned back to her and almost jumped over the table. Instead of a woman in a dress, a glowing figure stood in front of me. Her form shifted and swayed in the same amber light as the nihil below. She reached down to the table and handed me a card. It was labeled "The Hunter" and had a being on the front encased in exotic armor. A knight from a dimension long removed from mine.

"Your boon is life, hunter, and when you see the darkest moment life shall be returned", she said. With that she faded to nothingness. The room was just an empty dank room with no light and no music. And somehow I could feel the lack of her presence there. She too was gone. I held the card up in the moonlight and saw the image clearly for a moment more, before it dissolved to dust. Lady knew how to make an exit.

Chapter Twenty

The dog and I left the old house without any problems. The entire neighborhood was quiet. Which was weird because this neighborhood always had shouting, car alarms, or something else going on. Everything seemed to be at peace. But now I had a bigger problem. Where would I find Marcus? Guess it was time to do the cop thing and burn the boot leather. Beating the streets still worked better than any computer detective. They had fancy names for it in the military back in the day. HUMINT for Human Intelligence versus SIGINT for Signal Intelligence. It basically came down to talking to people versus using computers to do your searching.

I sat and thought about it for a minute. Most of the interactions I'd had with Marcus had been in and around Kernersville. I imagined a map in my mind and put a pin in each location mentally. With a modern criminal that wouldn't have meant as much with multiple highways running through the area and the availability of subtle things like cars, but I was betting a walking ghoul like Marcus wasn't as comfortable with modern means. I just felt he'd stick to a certain geographic location. But wouldn't he return to a crypt in Old Salem to hide from the sun my subconscious asked. He's not a literal ghoul I told it so it would shut up. Not discounting my subconscious I then added that to my mental map. It was a powerful tool much stronger than the logical mind.

Ok, so who would know the creepy and bizarre in that area? Gus would know. He was a serious slimeball and into some weird shit. I'd caught him one time trying to sell porn to a group of necrophiliacs. It was cut rate zombie porn but he tried to market it to a real group of weird folks. I'm not kink shaming but there were limits. Last I'd heard Gus stayed in a crack house near Burke St. It was an easy place to fence whatever he'd stolen or pick up odd items. I headed that way. I knew Gus would be active about this time of night, trying to close whatever shady deals he had going so he could get his bottle and bed down.

"Keep an eye out for a stringy nasty white male", I told Dog. "He always wears a jean jacket. If you have to bite him I'll probably have to take you to the ED for shots. There's no telling what you might catch from him." He growled a little as I turned onto Burke St. About a quarter mile after the turn Dog barked at a figure stumbling down the side of the road. I looked as we started to pass the figure and sure as hell it was Gus.

"Good job", I yelled but Dog wasn't there. As soon as he'd seen the figure he'd managed to hit the button to roll down the passenger side window and leapt out of the moving car and directly onto Gus. I slammed on the breaks and backed up. As I got out of the vehicle all I could hear was a very threatening growl and a wheezing whine. The whine was emanating from Gus. Dog stood between his shoulder blades pinning the nasty bastard to the ground. Dog's fur stood on end and he looked like what he was. A Hellhound, a hunter of men and souls. His eyes glinted a soft red in the night.

"Gus, long time no see", I said as I jauntily sauntered over to them.

"Detective Magnus", gus wheezed the question.

"Not a detective anymore Gus", I said.

"If this is about that pizza, I swear I was going to pay for it", he said.

"Nope, it's not about a pizza you tip stiffing ass", I growled.

"Then why is this thing on me", he asked.

"Because I want to talk to you and you have a habit of being difficult", I told him.

"That's slander, or whatever you call it", he said. "I have rights".

"You have rights that protect you from the government", I said. "I'm a private citizen. Your rights don't mean shit now", I said and leaned my butt on the car.

"Fuck you", he yelled.

"No thanks, you're not my type", I told him. "Now, I'm looking for someone".

"Who", he demanded.

"Dark hair, six footish, thin but not sick, wears black, goes by the name of Marcus", I said. Gus got real quiet. He didn't even move.

"Is he still alive", I asked Dog. Dog looked at me like I was stupid.

"Are you going to kill him", Gus asked.

"Why", I wanted to know.

"Fucker's been luring away kids. Maybe they're junkies, maybe not, but they're just kids. He takes them and no one sees them again", he said.

"You knew some of them", I asked. I was wondering about that room full of bodies and hoping none of them had been found there.

"Girl, went by Trish", he wheezed. "Hard luck story but she was a good kid. Marcus promised he'd give her a better life. I told her not to go but she didn't listen. Ain't nobody seen her since." He sounded like he was crying.

"Dog", I said. He understood and let Gus sit up. Gus looked worse than normal. Stringy hair and a sallow face with the red nose of the heavy drinker. He was a sad case for a man, but that was his choice. He told me once that he'd had money and a good family, but he'd rather be a drunk and liked living this way.

"So where do I find him", I asked.

"Promise you'll kill him", he said.

"I promise", I said. I would never have made such a promise to him but I didn't figure there'd be any evidence to link me to the murder anyway so what would it matter?

"You know the old place that group of motorcycle guys converted into their hangout somewhere around Old Valley School Rd", he asked.

"Yeah, it used to be an old store or something, right", I asked.

"Yeah, he's staying there. Rumors say he's staying there because there's a graveyard behind it. One of those really old one's without headstones. Guy is seriously creepy."

"Thank you", I told him and headed back to the car.

"You promised", he shouted at me. "Remember, for Trish, you promised." I drove off. It wouldn't be just for Trish but I'd add her name to the list.

I still had the vest and shotgun Lila had lent to me. I also had all my blades and my Glock 43 so I figured I could handle whatever I found. The place Gus was talking about was only a few minutes drive from Burke St. and I figured now was as good a time as any.

The old store sat along a dark stretch of road. There weren't many houses on that stretch and the night covered everything in an illusion of stillness. Someone had recently shot out the streetlight in front of the store so everything was blanketed in darkness. I stopped on the side of the road a couple of hundred feet from the place and shut off the car. Dog looked a question at me but I motioned for him to stay. A big mistake was to rush in instead of letting the environment settle and get a feel for everything around you. Better to go slow and live. After the night had settled we got out of the car.

I didn't see any lights coming from inside so we headed around back, sticking close to the treeline and moving slowly. I'd feel really great tripping over an old toilet or stepping into a hole. Hey, it's happened, at least the toilet did. We settled near the corner so we could see the back and side of the store. Flickering light came from inside. I waited a few minutes before moving up. We crossed the empty backyard and I found a crack in the plywood which covered most of the windows. Inside Marcus stood naked leaning over a wooden table. He was covered in blood, his thick black hair slicked back with it. It streaked down his muscular chest and along his arms. There was a woman lying nude on the table. He had cut open her chest and her bare ribs pointed at the ceiling. One full breast drooped towards the table lying pillowed on her arm as her chest cavity was spread wide open. She was nude as well. Marcus raised a wicked knife from where he had been doing something inside her chest and licked the edge of the blade. I was very thankful that I couldn't see how happy he was to be there. Other body parts from other victims hung from the walls around him.

I wanted to scream. I wanted to shoot him and burn the place down around his corpse. But I waited, waited to understand. Marcus removed the woman's body and flung it carelessly to the floor. The meaty thump of her body hitting the floor wasn't nearly as bad as watching her organs spill out. Marcus scooped a flame from the candle and placed the bare flame on the table. It hovered just above the table top. I could hear him muttering in a language I didn't know and the flame grew. When it was about a foot high and maybe eight inches around his voice changed. It became darker and more commanding. My gorge rose in my throat. He placed the heart within the fire and a horrible smell erupted from inside. The heart sizzled and burned and the fire turned from a yellow color to a dark sickly green. It solidified into a small purple and green pulsing light and I knew what I was looking at. Marcus had created a nihil. I knew I had to stop him but I didn't know how. I looked around and saw several fuel cans. A bonfire might make things better after all, I mean who doesn't like 'smores?

I moved quickly and carefully to get the cans which were still capped and full of what I hoped was fuel. I turned back to the building and found a true blessing. The place had a propane tank, maybe two hundred and fifty gallons, beside the rear entrance. The night was looking up!

I poured two cans of fuel around the rear of the building and on the walls as quietly as possible as Dog watched the back door for me. I placed two more sealed cans directly up against the monster propane tank. Dog and I pulled back into the trees. And I mean way back.

I could still see flickering shadows so I felt confident Marcus was still inside. I drew my Glock 43 and braced my arm against a tree. This was a really long shot for the short barreled pistol but I took my time and really lined up the shot. Breath, pause, squeeze, and can we say boom?

That propane tank must have had way more in it than I thought. The resulting blast knocked me on my ass from forty feet away. Half the structure, including the rear of the building, was gone. But not for long. Fiery chunks began raining down from the sky. I slowly approached the building looking for pieces of Marcus. I couldn't hear shit and I'd need to call it in soon so I could pretend to be a witness. I could smell burning meat and small pieces of body parts littered the ground. From inside a barely standing doorway a figure stepped out. It was horribly burned, half its face burned away. The figure was holding its left arm up to its shoulder and thick ropey tendrils formed and pulled the arm back onto the body. Similar tendrils were rebuilding the face and broken parts of the body. I guess I knew how he had survived the gunshot blasts. I knew my pistol wouldn't do any good and I didn't bring the shotgun. I drew Lilas knife from my back and moved into the burning rubble. Marcus saw me and grinned his death's head grin.

"Soon Mr. Magnus, but not this day", he said and snapped the fingers on his good hand. The nihil he had conjured spread from the floor and enveloped him before burning with a bright green light and fading to nothing. He was gone. He had gotten away again! Oh I was going to kill that son of a bitch!

Chapter Twenty
One

Dog and I made it back to the car and drove off before the first responders showed up. I didn't know what I'd do next, but I knew I had to get out of here. The trick to this was going to be to drive normally. The adrenaline hits and you want to run. That's the best way to get caught. Driving slowly and carefully, without a care in the world, draws less attention. I maintained the speed limit and stopped fully at all stop signs. Nothing to see here folks.

I had burned my lead and Marcus had escaped again. If the application of explosives didn't stop him I was going to have to get real serious about our hate-hate relationship. Maybe if I sealed him in concrete? Or maybe a steel coffin and we dump it in the Marianas Trench? I was going to need more information. Dog and I made it home safe and I grabbed a shower while he raided the fridge. I sat in the living room and fumed and thought. I slowly put patterns together in my head, small pieces forming bigger pictures, associations from bits of information.

"Well shit", I finally said. Dog looked at me. "We're going to have to go see the one woman I was hoping we wouldn't need to drag into this". He cocked his head at me.

"We'll go in the morning", I told him. "Do you want a name", I asked randomly. He growled at me showing me his canines. Ok, no name, at least for right now. I held up my hands in surrender and headed to the bedroom. Dog came and joined me as I got settled and it didn't take long for either of us to drift off to sleep.

I was standing on the sidewalk in a sunny neighborhood. It could have been any suburb anywhere. A gentle wind stirred the trees and the voices of kids sounded nearby. The scene was the definition of a peaceful day. And then I heard sirens. I watched immobile as Sam, Clara, and several faceless deputies rolled up to a house. The house had appeared normal at first. But now I could see it was covered in bodies. Bodies nailed to the eaves and hanging by the neck from the gutters. Body parts littered the front yard. The house was covered in death. Clara and Sam took up positions behind their vehicles. I could feel a small hand intertwine itself with my own. I looked down to see the little girl, her head fully attached for once, holding my hand.

She smiled up at me, but it was a very sad smile. I looked back in time to see what happened next. Sam and Clara were yelling orders at the house. The front door opened and Marcus stepped out. Marcus moved slowly, smirking at the drawn guns like they didn't matter. And to him they didn't.

Marcus raised both hands to the sky. The true blue sky was eaten by a black vortex. Purple lightning ate through the air around the vortex as it grew. Sam and Clara stood motionless staring up into that blackness. Like some evil priest Marcus stood laughing with those muscular arms raised above his head rejoicing in the evil he had unleashed.

"One of them will die", the little girl said. I looked down at her and then snapped my head back up in time to see the ropes of malevolent energy streak from the sky towards Sam and Clara. I tried to yell, tried to scream but no sound came out. I tried to run towards them but my body wouldn't move. I screamed raggedly in my mind as the lightning reached them.

I woke up as I landed on the floor. The impact was jarring as I lay all piled up on the ancient carpet. I was still sobbing as I realized it had been a dream. Except it was never just a dream when she showed up. The dog huffed from on top of the bed and a pillow landed on top of me. I guess he was kicking me out of bed. Her words haunted me. "One of them will die".

We had slept till just after noon so it was time to head out. I called Sam first. I knew that the person I needed to see at the library wouldn't be in till after four. The phone rang three times before Sam answered.

"What's up Cy", he asked.

"I was hoping to drop by and check on you", I said.

"And to question Nina", he said.

"Well, I didn't want it to seem like that", I told him.

"We're still cops Cy, it was obvious", he said and laughed. "Do you have any leads?"

"Not many", I told him. I was not going to tell him that I had blown my only lead trying to blow up the bad guy. It wouldn't inspire confidence. Besides, he'd pick on me for the next twenty years about it. You know, after he got done having an aneurysm because I had let the guy who had kidnapped his daughter get away. Somehow I did not think he would take it well.

"Cy, you're better than this", he said.

"So, mind if I drop by", I asked again. I didn't want him involved. If that meant that he had to think I was falling down on the job, then so be it.

"Yeah, Nina's been asking for you all morning anyway", he said. "She says she's got something she'll only show to you". He didn't sound happy about that.

"I'm on the way", I told him. I went over to the bed to get Dog. He was huge! He had grown again while we slept and he was the size of a large mastiff.

"Did I fall off the bed or did you push me", I asked him. He just rolled out his tongue and panted a little. I had a strong suspicion I had been pushed.

"Come on", I told him. He took his time getting up and stretching. He was obviously not impressed with me or my desires. I opened the door and he trotted out on his own time. Must be his teenage years.

We headed back over to Sam and Betty's. The cold was even more intense today with dark gray clouds marring the sky. The little car had an amazing heater but I didn't think we'd get warm even if we set a fire in the back seat. We finally made it to Sam's before frostbite set in. Even Dog looked frozen and he had his own fur. Wonder if he'd bite me if I tried to get him a sweater?

"Is that the same dog", Sam asked from the doorway.

"Yep", I said.

"What kind of food are you giving him", he asked.

"Raw meat", I said with a grin. Sam held his hand down to Dog and was nearly bowled over when Dog jumped up on his chest and licked Sam's face before barging into Sam's home. He gave Betty a small lick as he headed to Nina's room. Betty came charging up to me and threw herself at me. She latched her arms around my neck and I held her while she cried.

"Thank you for saving her", she kept saying. I held her for a few minutes until she had gotten it all out.

"Cy's here to talk to Nina", Sam told her.

"Of course, just go easy on her Cy", Betty said. "We haven't asked but...", Betty trailed off.

"Hey, she's my family too", I told them.

"We know", Betty said. I headed back to Nina's room. I stood outside her door for a minute and reconsidered. She wasn't a little girl anymore. Did I really need to be in her bedroom? This could be weird.

"Come in Cy", she called. Of course she knew I was standing out here. I pushed open the door. Dog was curled up with her on her bed. There was a crazy contrast in the young goth girl on the bed with my dog and the teenage girls room that surrounded us. The room was as bright and cheerful as her dress was not. I shut the door behind me but I'd be damned if I was going to sit on her bed. I found a small chair by her desk and perched there.

"So, what's up", she asked.

"How are you feeling", I asked.

"A little scared", she said. "A little stupid."

"Everyone makes mistakes hon", I told her.

"He just seemed so charming", she said. "And he knew the answers to my questions. He said he'd show me the world in a way no one had ever seen. He made me feel like...", she stopped.

"Like a woman", I asked.

"Yeah", she said and blushed a little.

"There's nothing wrong with that Nina", I told her.

"Except that he was a psycho who kidnapped me", she said.

"Well, you probably missed a few red flags", I told her. She snorted at me. "At least you didn't fall for the free candy gag", I told her, trying to cheer her up. She flipped me off. That was my girl!

"Nina", I said, "I do need to know a few things".

"Like what", she asked and burrowed further into Dog.

"Did Marcus say anything about where he would be? What he was looking for or who", I asked.

"There's a book behind you", she said. "Before he tied me up he gave me a paper to read from. But I couldn't make out the words. He flipped out when I couldn't read it but I managed to save the paper. He was ranting at me about helping him stop you Cy. Why does he want to stop you?"

"Probably because I'm looking to throw him one hell of an ass beating", I told her. I found the book on the desk and pulled out the sheet of paper. There definitely was some kind of writing on it, but the letters kept moving and squiggling around on the paper. I couldn't read it, but I bet Lila could.

"Did he say anything that might help me find him", I asked.

"No, it was all ramblings. Stuff about his family, some moravian graveyard, weird stuff", she told me.

"Ok hon, thank you", I told her.

"You're welcome Cy", she said. "I hope you get him."

"Oh I will", I told her. And I would, somehow. I left her room and came back to the living room to say my goodbyes. Sam and Betty were waiting for me. Sam sat holding Betty on the couch. She was still crying gently.

"Did you get anything", Sam asked.

"Not much", I told him. I wasn't lying, it wasn't much.

"So what now", he asked.

"You stay here with your family and keep them safe. I go do what I do best", I said.

"You're going to need help", he said.

"I've got someone in mind", I told him. "I won't play Lone Ranger on this one". Which was true, because I had already tried that and failed. Otherwise, well nevermind.

"I can help", Sam said.

"No you cannot", Betty said and stood up. She was about to go toe to toe with the magnificent giant and my money was on Betty. "You will stay here and keep us safe until Cy gives us the all clear, do you hear me?"

"I hear you", he said and sighed.

"Can you two do that again so I can film it", I asked. "You know, for science?"

"Cy", Betty said and turned on me. "Get out there and get the man who took my daughter."

"Yes ma'am", I said. From nowhere Dog came running to join me. We headed out. I was really dreading going to the library. I loved libraries but it was more who I'd be there to see. I didn't even know if she'd help me. Sometimes she could stand me and sometimes I thought she'd stab me if given half the chance. This should be fun.

Chapter Twenty
Two

Dog and I got to the Central Library about thirty minutes before closing time. We'd stopped at a taco truck on Fourth St and loaded up on burritos. Dog was a sloppy eater but good company. I loved the ambiance at Central. It was a mix of Nineteen Sixties construction with furniture from the Nineteen Eighties. The exterior was your standard concrete and glass facade of the infamous governmental building. The inside was made up of safety glass and wooden furniture that had seen more abuse over its time than a professional fighter. It was a time capsule of of an era that wanted to be better and just wasn't.

You could find all types of people here. It seemed like every strata of Americana moved through this building at one time or another. The city kept making plans to tear it down and build something more modern, but I hoped they never did. Most everyone stayed on the first floor but Dog and I needed to meet someone on the second. We went through the lobby and then up the central staircase to the North Carolina room. It was a pretentious name but it was where a lot of the local historical documents were kept.

We walked over to the librarian help desk. The desk was all stained wood and brass. It was a beautiful display of class from when craftsmanship was still a real thing. The young man behind the desk looked up at me. He wore a little name tag proclaiming him to be Brian. His parents must have been proud. He looked at me strangely enough that I could tell not many people came up here anymore.

"Can I help you", Brian asked.

"Absolutely. I'm looking for Hana", I told him with my best smile. He looked confused.

"I'm sorry, who", he asked.

"Hanna Rein", I told him. "She was the Chief Librarian of this section".

"Oh, yes, sorry. Ms. Rein, of course", he said. I don't think he had ever heard her first name. "May I ask what this is in regards to", he asked with an empty smile.

"It's a research project concerning boudoir calisthenic patterns of the early nineteen hundreds", I said pretentiously. When in doubt, baffle them with bullshit.

"Of course, one moment", he said and picked up the phone. Poor guy had no idea I was yanking his chain. That was absolutely no fun. He spoke into the phone for a moment and then set it down.

"She'll be right out", he said helpfully. I thanked him and walked over to a display of old farm tools. These had been rescued from Bethabra, a local settlement which was still being explored and preserved in Northern Forsyth County. I always loved stuff like this. It was a visual link to what came before us. An old scythe caught my attention and I just couldn't imagine the level of labor it took to carve out a life with such tools.

The entire second floor was populated with displays of artifacts and maps. Portraits were framed on the walls of people long dead who had helped found the county. Old and modern books lined shelf after shelf preserving history that was almost lost. It was an amazing place to be. I saw a shadow coalesce in the reflection on the glass case. I was almost startled but then I realized Hanna was moving up behind me. Probably for a killing blow.

"Hello Hanna", I said without turning around.

"Why are you here", she demanded.

"It's good to see you're always so welcoming", I told her as I turned to face her. Her blonde white hair was piled atop her head very neatly. Her glasses framed her beautiful eyes to make them more striking. She had really pale skin but it suited her. A dark business suit skirt hugged her full lithesome body. Dark patterned hose kissed amazing legs and I knew there would be full garters underneath. Everything Hanna wore breathed sophistication.

"Why are you here", she asked again. Guess she wasn't up for the witty banter portion of the encounter.

"I need your help catching the guy who kidnapped Sam's daughter", I said. I knew that would make her stop.

"Is she still missing", Hanna asked.

"I got her back and she's home safe, but she's not the only one in danger. This guy is a stone cold murderer and has killed a lot of people", I told her.

"I didn't know you were back on the job", she said.

"This is unofficial", I told her. "Feel free and call Murphy, he'll back me up", I said.

"I stopped helping the cops a long time ago, Cy", she said. And she had. Murphy, Sam, and I had come to her with a murder case. She'd been targeted by the killer. He broke into her house one night and I'd gotten there just in time. She was still mad at me for spreading his brains over her designer duvet. But she was an innocent who should have never been on his radar.

"This one's different", I told her.

"Are you different",she asked.

"Yeah, yeah I am now", I said and looked down at the floor.

"I'm sorry about you and the wife", she said.

"It was a rough thing, all of it was", I told her. The problem was, I'd known Hanna since she was a baby librarian and I was a rookie. We'd always had this crazy attraction and could spend hours talking, but we agreed early that we would never act on it. It was kinda my fault she had been pulled into a messy hunt for a messier killer.

"Show me what you've got", she said. "I'll at least take a look."

"Can we talk in private", I asked. "This may seem kinda crazy".

"Of course it's going to seem crazy", she said, "you're involved. Now spill or leave". She crossed her arms over her chest. I pulled out the note Nina had given me and showed it to her. She blanched.

"Follow me", she said. Dog got up and followed us out. He gave me a hubba hubba look as Hanna started down the stairs.

"Tell your dog to keep his eyes in his head", she said over her shoulder.

"You can see him", I asked.

"He's huge Cy, of course I can see him", she replied.

I thought she would head to her office but she led me to a rear stairwell. We went down to the basement and started walking through racks and shelves of old books. After maybe a hundred feet through a maze of cobwebs and damaged books we came to the door of what had been an old office. It had wood panels down low but the upper half of the outer wall was all glass. Someone had painted over the glass from the inside so that no one could peer in. Hanna opened the door and ushered us inside. I walked in and stopped in shock.

The interior walls were covered floor to ceiling in well cared for books. Some of them were way older than this library. The room was warmly lit with old bankers lamps on deeply stained oaken tables. In the center of the room sat a large stone urn or bowl on top of a beautiful wooden table, both of which were intricately carved.

"Wow, nice digs", I told her. And then I stopped. I hadn't noticed at first but some of the books were glowing. Others towards the very back of the room had been chained to the bookshelves because they were trying to float away. They pulsed with different colors and some even gave off the feeling of being malevolent. I focused and looked around again. Everything in the room had an aura of some sort. How had I not noticed before? Hanna was standing near the door watching me. Dog walked in and laid down under one of the tables.

"So you can see it now", she said.

"Whether I want to or not", I told her.

"For how long", she asked.

"For about a week. It started with my nightmares, then all kinds of other things. I've got this real evil guy hunting me and everyone around me. I've tried to stop him twice and he just gets up and walks away. I need to know everything I can before he kills more people", I explained.

"And before he kills you", she said.

"I'm not sure if he wants to kill me, own me, or fuck me; but yeah", I said. She burst out laughing.

"You never change", she gasped, "I love that.

"At your service", I said and bowed.

"So I'm assuming that whatever you saw on that paper is why we're down here", I asked.

"What, I couldn't have brought you down here to seduce you", she asked.

"Nah, I've never been that lucky", I said back. She laughed again.

"I can't read the writing on the paper", she said, "but I have seen something like it before." She went through the shelves and lifted a huge volume from the stacks. She brought it to the table near me and slammed it down. To be fair she may not have slammed it, it was probably as heavy as a couch. She started flipping through the pages until she came to a picture.

"This your guy", she asked. I moved closer to her to see the picture. Our shoulders and hips were touching as I looked. It was a drawing of a family. A man, woman, and two girls stood in the portrait in period clothing. And damn if the man wasn't Marcus. I didn't mean it looked like him, it was him. Period.

"That's him", I said.

"I thought as much. The portrait doesn't list his name. But there is an interesting story about this family. It was hidden from the official histories to prevent bad gossip from going around. The man was a soldier before he immigrated. His wife was some kind of healer or nurse. He apparently found religion before immigrating. Some of the stories say he was forced to immigrate because he felt killing in the name of his god was righteous.", she told me.

"Let me guess, he started being a little too righteous", I asked.

"That sums it up. He settled here in Salem and wanted to be a deacon but the town fathers kept refusing him. Then one day he slaughtered his entire family. Brutally slaughtered them. He's found by a stable hand wearing his wife's entrails like a Mardi Gras necklace. They tried to capture him but he killed everyone who was sent after him. He finally fled towards the Peter's Creek area and vanished from the histories", she said.

"Is that where the stories end", I asked.

"Yes and no", she said. "There are stories of these things, like portals, in the local lore. Of course it's from the same time that the local indigenous population supposedly walked side by side with Sasquatch along Peter's Creek so anything's possible. At any rate, some of the stories claim he killed his family as a sacrifice to open one of these portals. Of course, a lot of this is hearsay, there aren't any facts that we can really identify. It could be true or it could all be rumor and superstition."

"And how do you know all this", I asked. She smirked at me. "Is there anything hotter than a sexy librarian and a book", she asked.

"No there is not", I said and bumped her hip with mine.

"Come here", she said and led me to another station. A really nice computer station had been set up on one of the desks. She hit a key and a website popped up. It was a page dedicated to the dark and occult history of Winston Salem and the surrounding area. She had a whole page dedicated to this one subject. About halfway down the page was a picture of carvings made into a tree. The writing was the same as on the slip of paper I had shown Hanna. There was another section below it.

"What's this", I asked.

"Well, in the late seventies or early eighties the legend of this guy resurfaced with a chilling hook", she said. "Local practitioners were claiming to have encountered him and that he was killing young people who had certain abilities. The person telling the story seemed to think he was killing them to absorb their power."

"Ok, good to know", I said. "Hey, have you ever heard the name Loros", I asked on a whim.

"Why",she asked.

"I met him and wanted to know if I needed to worry about him", I said.

"You met Loros the Shadow King", she said. She obviously thought I was making it up.

"Yes, thank you very much", I said.

"Well then you have nothing to worry about", she said.

"I don't", I asked.

"Nope, you are way too small a fish for a Shadow King to worry about", she said with a laugh. From under the table Dog snorted in mirth.

"But, if you're worried", she said, "then take this for luck." She reached up and grabbed me by the collar of my shirt. She pulled me down and kissed me violently. Before I could react she had pushed me away.

"Time for you to go", she said and pushed me out the door of the office. I stood confused for a minute and the door opened long enough for Dog to trot out and join me before shutting again. He looked at me with eyes full of mirthful pity before heading up the steps and out the rear door. I followed him. We headed the two blocks back to my car in the frigid dark. Downtown was beautiful at night but I was too confused to enjoy it. I must not have been paying attention because when I hit the key fob to unlock the doors I saw a figure standing by the passenger door.

"Looks like you had a good day", Lila said to me. Damn, was there lipstick?

Chapter Twenty Three

"I'm sorry", I questioned.

"You survived going after Marcus without me", she said. "I'd say that was a good day."

"I thought I had him", I told her. Dog barked at us and I opened the door so he could get in out of the wind. Lila opened the passenger side door and got in as well. I followed, it was my car after all.

"But you did not", she said.

"Look, very few problems cannot be fixed with the proper application of explosives. No one told me he was bomb proof", I said.

"Then let me tell you now, Marcus is proof against mortal weapons", she said. "Nothing that you have known thus far will harm him."

"Well that's just wonderful", I said. Lila snorted at me.

"So what do we use", I asked.

"I believe I gave you a knife, did I not", she asked.

"You did", I said.

"And do you have it", she asked.

"Yeah, it's in a spine sheath on my lower back", I said.

"Good", she said with a smile. "You will need it."

"Oh, why, do you know where Marcus is", I asked.

"No, but it is time for you to prepare", she said.

"Prepare", I asked. "Prepare how?"

"Warriors of old would take on a quest to grow stronger and find balance. It prepared them for their battles. A simple quest could rehone their awareness, tune their reflexes so they were prepared for any challenge. You need to center yourself in your abilities, find yourself on this new battlefield," she told me.

"And why can't we just do the rational thing and keep tracking Marcus", I asked.

"Have you had any luck killing him so far", she asked. I opened my mouth to protest and shut it again. I didn't like it but she had a point. I really didn't want to take time for side quests. We needed to be focused on the problem.

"Give me one night", she said.

"One night then you help me find him and kill him", I said.

"It will be a very long night to accomplish all in one attempt", she said. "The challenge will be very difficult."

"Well, we'll just have to do it live", I said.

"I don't understand", she replied.

"You had to have been there", I told her. "Where to first."

"We need to find Marcus's grave", she said. "It's in a crypt in Old Salem."

"Of course it would be", I said.

We drove for about twenty minutes in the dark. I had an idea on where to stash the car and it wasn't too hard to meander into the graveyard at night. But if this would weaken Marcus, help us bring him down, then we were on the right track.

I parked in a little lot near Salem College and the greenway through the graveyard. No one would think anything of us parking here. Lila put her arm in mine and Dog frollicked around as we walked the greenway. Nothing to see here, just a couple taking their dog for a walk. We headed into the graveyard and towards the crypts.

"Keep a lookout for security", I told Dog.

"Are you ever going to name him", Lila asked. Dog growled at her gently.

"Yeah, I asked him", I said. "I don't think he wants one." Dog loped off.

"Which way", I asked.

"I believe it's in the oldest part, where all the statues are", she said. I headed down the hill to that section of the graveyard. It was dark and now it was starting to snow. Yay, not only would we be cold, we'd soon be wet and cold. We could be naked under fur blankets by Lilas fire, but no, we were here hunting the desecrated grave of a homicidal mad man. Yep, this was my life!

This part of the cemetery was as creepy and gothic as one could wish. Statues of several varieties dotted the landscape and beautiful crypts stood decedent in the night. Old cobblestones had been grown over leaving the ground uneven. I felt like I saw movement out of the corner of my eye and turned to look. The stone angel stood dancing on its pedestal. It moved with soft grace in the moonlight. Specters hovered around the statue, dancing in time to the stone angels movements in the night. As it danced I saw the faces of the dead, joyous for one moment, free from the loneliness of being forgotten in their graves. The wind blew strongly and I turned back to the path. From behind a gravestone a spectral shape sprang out, holding its hands out like it was going to grab me. I fell backward onto the cold ground and yelped.

"Do you always scream like a girl", Lila asked, laughing.

"Ha Ha", I said back, not enjoying the cold ground and having landed on it.

"It's just a haint", she said and offered me a hand up.

"Yeah, and it scared the shit out of me", I told her. She dusted the dirt off me as I straightened up. "Thank you", I said. We were standing very close to each other and her face was turned up to me. I leaned down to kiss her. Her mouth looked so inviting. Dog barked behind us, snapping us out of the moment. He was sitting by an open crypt door.

"You couldn't have waited", I asked him. He huffed at me.

"This is it. It has to be", she said and walked over to examine the lock. All the crypts were chained shut to prevent vandalism, so this one standing open was a clue.

"Asshole", I whispered as I walked past Dog. He gently nipped at my ankle as I passed. The name above the crypt door had been weathered to illegibility. But there were glyphs carved on the outer edge of each door. The glyphs moved and writhed on their own. Yep, this was it. I pulled out my little flashlight.

"Think anyone's in there", I asked.

"Only one way to find out", she said and walked inside. Damned fool. I followed her in checking the corners and the ceiling. It'd be just my luck something creepy was attached to the roof waiting to drop down like a spider from hell. The crypt was granite polished to smooth stone. It had been constructed well after the time of Marcus's family's deaths. Maybe he'd had the crypt built and the bodies moved? The walls gave back tiny echoes every time we moved. There was a small barred window in the back letting in a hint of moonlight and a bier or table near the front entrance. There were fresh flowers in the urns on three of the grave placards. Someone had been here recently.

I looked at the names etched on the burial plaques but they had been worn off as well. I had hoped if we could come up with a last name we might get closer to the truth of Marcus's past. But one of the plagues was sitting on the floor leaving an inky black hole in the already dark crypt.

"Lila", I said, "come take a look at this."

"What did you find", she asked, coming over to me from the bier.

"Looks like it's Marcus's grave", I said. Lila stopped moving. The look on her face concerned me. She slowly reached to the small of her back and drew her knife. It glowed with a light all its own, making her face look demonaic in the small crypt.

"Lila", I asked again but she didn't respond. My thoughts raced back to Loros's comment about neither of them being wholly good or evil. Had I made a bad tactical error? Was Lila just as much my enemy as Marcus and I had fallen for a sexy package? She stood absolutely still. I waited, if she attacked I'd defend myself, but I didn't have enough information to judge.

"Move", Lila shouted. I moved. A dark shadow coalesced from inside the open hole in the wall of the crypt. In seconds it had formed itself from ethereal smoke into a large figure in a black cloak. Where the face and hands should be was just as black. A stygian scythe formed in the things hands. Lila threw her knife, impaling the thing through the chest just to the left of where it's sternum would be.

I dug in my pocket, a sudden thought hitting me. Deep in the pocket of my leather jacket I found what I needed. I drew out a small bottle of herbs and threw them onto the specter. It froze, unable to move. Which surprised me as I really thought it would drive the thing off.

"What was that", Lila demanded.

"Something called Hot Powder", I said.

"Is it supposed to make the specter hot", she asked.

"Nevermind", I said, "why are we being attacked by a grim reaper wannabe?"

"Let's ask", she said and moved closer.

"Why did you attack us", she demanded from the specter.

"The sorcerer compels me", it hissed. It's voice echoed and slithered around the crypt. Magnifying itself from the walls and ground.

"How", I asked.

"There is a spell written inside the grave", it said.

"Carved into the coffin, on paper, what", I asked.

"On flesh, hungry flesh, inside the grave", it hissed. I looked at Lila and shrugged. She took my flashlight and moved around the specter carefully. I kept an eye on it as she dug in the hole. She pulled out something brown and leathery with the same moving sigils on it as the piece of paper and the entrance to the crypt. She showed it to me.

"Is that...", I started to ask.

"Human skin", she said.

"Ugh", I said.

"Free me", it demanded.

"You just tried to kill us", I said.

"Not of its own accord Cy", Lila said. "Your kind, you can corrupt graves", she asked.

"Yes", it hissed. It was trying to struggle against the powder but wasn't getting very far.

"Can you make them whole again", she asked.

"For a price", the sibilant voice said.

"I will free you, destroy this spell, if you will restore the sanctity of this crypt and all who have resided herein. From there you will be allowed to leave in peace", she told the specter.

"Agreed", it said in a wheeze.

"Cy, go stand at the entrance please", she said. I did what she asked. One of us needed to have a clue as to what was going on. It sure wasn't me.

Lila took off her jacket and swung it through the air blowing enough of the powder off the thing that it could move. She then reached up and withdrew her knife from it's chest. It grew in size, swelling up to take more space. Lila stood waiting. I had the impression she didn't care whether it kept its word or attacked.

It turned and examined each grave carefully. Then it plunged its dark hand into its breast and drew out an orb of light. The orb shimmered and glowed like a fire opal.

The specter tapped the top of the orb and it split into four parts. The specter placed each piece against a burial plaque, which absorbed the orb. The last piece the specter placed inside Marcus's open grave. Black energy shot out of the hole in every direction, bouncing from the walls and ceiling. It ricocheted in every direction before plunging out of the small window in the crypt and into the night. The specter turned back to us and bowed. Then it turned to me.

"My master sends his regards", it told me. Somehow I just knew who its master had to be.

"Please return my compliments to Loros", I told the specter. It bowed again and then faded into the blackness.

"You make friends in strange places", Lila said.

"Hey better friends in low places", I joked. I had a hunch that there was still something that needed to be done.

"Hey, I want to try something", I told her.

"What", she asked.

I reached deep inside myself while pushing my senses outwards at the same time. It was kinda weird to be honest, but I wanted to try. I focused until I felt a familiar energy nearby. I pulled the energy to me. A small glowing nihil appeared within the crypt. I turned and looked at the three closed graves. A woman and two teenage girls stood clutching one another in front of the plaques.

"It's ok", I told them, "you're free." They moved forward into the nihil, moving on from their restless time dead. They were free to move on, away from Marcus, away from this dimension. I hoped they ended up somewhere better. I let the nihil close behind them.

"That was impressive", Lila said.

"Hey, I've got skills", I told her. We exited the crypt and I helped Lila push the crypt door closed. We couldn't chain it back together, but we could close it. Maybe that would be good enough.

I turned and faced Lila in the gentle moonlight. She stood looking at me, maybe considering me. I gently stepped forward and slowly kissed her. She moved into the kiss, parting her lips and welcoming me. And this time we didn't have interference.

Chapter Twenty
Four

We walked back from the graveyard arm in arm again. This time it wasn't just a cover. We weren't just pretending to accomplish a mission. For these few minutes we meant every second of it. Neither of us knew if we'd be alive in a day or three. Better make the most of the time we had.

"Where to now", I asked her.

"Are you familiar with Washington Park", she asked.

"At night", I asked. The park was in a borderline rough area. A few years before the city had tried to clean it up and had succeeded pretty well. But it was still not the best place to be after dark.

"After all you've seen and now you're afraid", she asked.

"I'm not afraid", I said, "but I'm also not into the cheap thrills thing either."

"This will not be a cheap thrill", she told me. I drove the few blocks to the park. She was in charge, I was just Tail End Charlie on this one. We parked on the side of the road. Yeah, I was parked illegally. But trust me, no one was getting out in this weather to write a parking citation. Besides, in this neighborhood, who would notice?

We entered the park and walked through the frozen grass and playground equipment. The snow had tapered off but the wind was cutting through my clothes like a pimp's straight razor and I couldn't feel my feet. This was so much fun. A while back a friend of mine and I were sitting watch in a far off land full of unfriendly people who wanted to kill us because of the uniforms we wore. He told me that he never thought Hell was hot like certain religions believed. He thought Hell was a frozen place so miserable the cold burned like fire. I was starting to wonder if we had arrived in his version of Hell after all. Maybe I'd see him here? I missed him, but then again, I missed all of them.

"There", Lila said, shocking me out of my reverie.

"Where", I asked.

"Do you see that copse of trees", she asked.

"Yeah", I said.

"Do you not find it odd that the trees are still green in this frozen month", she asked. As she said it, it was like the thought dawned on me. I had never noticed before. My breath steamed from my mouth as I let out a little sigh.

"So now what", I asked.

"You go in and Dog and I will wait here", she said.

"Why aren't you coming with me", I asked.

"Because some things must be done alone", she said. That answer sucked ass so much. But whatever, I just wanted this done so I could get warm again.

I headed to the copse of trees. The wind got colder the closer I got. The swaying trees gave me an illusion of moving shadows under the trees. I hoped it was an illusion anyway. I stepped onto the path between the trees expecting something to grab me and drag me kicking into the trees. All I'd probably see was a couple of homeless guys or a wandering junkie trying to find a place to shoot up, but imagination is a powerful thing.

The darkness felt oppressive. If depression had a color, it was the shadows under those trees. I just felt so hopeless and alone. Why was I bothering? I always failed to save the people I cared about. I was always too late. Why keep fighting? Was it worth it anymore?

I shook my head and refused to let the pull of the helplessness take me. It was like a riptide and if I gave in I'd drown in it. I'd swum through every part of that ocean and nothing good had ever come from it. I could quit or I could fight. And every moment, every second was a choice to keep moving, keep fighting, keep living. I headed along the path.

I had learned a long time ago that my flashlight would only make it harder to see in that kind of darkness so I left it in my pocket. My natural eyesight would serve me way better in the dark. As I moved deeper I could hear things rustling around me. There's always noise anywhere that there's nature. But the noises were coming from every direction and sounded heavier than branches or possums could make. Which did not bode well for little old me. There was a clearing ahead. I could just make out a figure struggling in the clearing. I moved to one side of the trail, closer to the trees to minimize my silhouette. The figure appeared to be a woman. I moved up to the mouth of the clearing but just at the edge of the trail and stopped to check the scene. There was a woman, thin and frail looking, suspended in the center of the clearing by dark ropes of energy. The energy ropes pulsed as if they were alive. She was hanging upside down, legs and arms splayed like an X. Her light colored hair hung loosely, the last little bit pooling on the ground. Shit, had someone tied her up like that?

I looked around carefully but I didn't see anyone in the clearing. I edged closer to the woman. She didn't appear to be hurt but that wasn't always visible in the dark. I got about three feet from her before her eyes snapped open. Her eyes glowed light green and she stared intently at me. A piece of the dark energy was covering her mouth so she couldn't speak. I figured it was a trap but the only way I could see to save her was to keep going. I'd deal with the ambush when it came.

The woman tried to speak, tried to yell, but no sound came out. I spun with my knife held low and ready as a form rushed at me. I stepped to the side of the charge and sliced upward making solid contact with my attacker. Blood flew from my blade and the smell of entrails greeted my nostrils. The figure slid to a halt beside the bound woman. It was hunched over and holding its gut. The figure looked up at me in the glimmer of light peeking through the trees.

Its face was horribly misshapen. One eye looked higher than the other and its nose had rotted off long ago. Boils oozed liquid from several places on its face. The things limbs hung at odd angles inside an oversized coat. Anyone would think it was just another homeless person if they ever saw it.

"Mine", it hissed. "Kill you."

I didn't waste time on banter. From the smell I'd opened up the thing's stomach. If I pressed the fight now I'd have a better chance. I moved in quickly and it raised clawed hands encased in old knit gloves, ready to defend itself. I feinted left then came in on the midline with the knife. Fire burned along the edge of the blade as I plunged it deep into the monster's chest. It clutched at me, its fingers scrabbling on my leather coat as it slowly died in my arms. That was the thing about knife fighting, you had to get real close. Which made killing anything really personal. And it should be personal. You were taking a life. It shouldn't be done by proxy. The creature fell to the ground giving its last few spasmodic twitches.

I stood trying to draw breath through my frozen lips, my knife hanging loosely in my hand. The woman's face looked terrified as blood dripped onto the earth near her head. I stood like that for a couple of moments, slowing my heart and controlling the adrenaline.

"Oh relax", I told her, "I'm not here to hurt you." I don't think she believed me. As I was trying to cryogenically preserve my lungs by breathing, she'd just have to wait a moment for me to be empathetic. The gray streamers were fading from my vision and I remembered to clean my knife before putting it in its sheath. It was a testament to the fact that I wasn't thinking as I realized I'd have to cut the woman down.

I drew the knife a second time and cut the black energy cords from her wrists first. They came apart with an audible hissing pop. Then I cut her left leg free. I tried to move quickly and keep her head from crashing into the ground as I cut the final rope. I steadied her the best I could as she tumbled to the ground, but there was only so much I could do. As soon as she hit the ground she scrambled a few feet back from me. I gave her the space as she reached up and ripped the final energy tendril from around her mouth. She gagged as she extracted a long proboscis of black energy from deep within her lungs and stomach. She just kept drawing the black rope out of her mouth until she had finally gotten it all out. She flung it to the edge of the clearing in disgust.

"You", she stopped and had to try again. "You are the one called Cy", she asked.

"That's me, yeah", I said. I had my arms crossed over my chest trying to find warmth.

"You saved me", she said.

"I did", I stated.

"Why", she asked.

"Seemed like the thing to do at the time", I said.

"Do not be flippant", she said. "Why did you risk your life for me?"

"Because you needed help and that's what I do. I help people", I told her. She smiled at me.

"So now we both know why you do what you do", she said. The import of what she said hit me in the gut. It was such a simple thing. But it was a truth. One of my truths. I helped people, sometimes even saved them, it was who I was. It was a part of me I'd refused to look at for a long time.

"Thank you for saving me too", she said. Her form grew hazy and indistinct. She looked more like mist than a person. Slowly that mist spread throughout the clearing and the barren earth was covered in moss and grass. It had been bare earth and now it was full of life. Life in the frigid heart of winter. Now that was impressive.

I backtracked along the path and back out to Lila. She was huddled on the ground with Dog. I guess they had decided to huddle for warmth. It was a smart thing to do. She looked up at me and smiled, her hair streaked with frost.

"Did you find what you needed", she asked.

"Yeah, I think I did", I told her. "What is she?"

A nature spirit, bound to the land", Lila told me. "Sometimes they can become poisoned and pollute the land. Other times they are captured and drained of their essence. Some things feed on energy such as hers."

"Well, she's safe for the moment at least", I said.

"Good", she said, "then let us warm up before our final stop."

"Hey, wouldn't it be better to find a warm shower and a warmer bed", I asked her. "You know, if we get up close under the covers we could warm each other."

"Not yet Cy", she said and laughed. "This is important".

"Important to who", I asked.

"To you", she said and started to walk away. I turned to Dog.

"Do you know what she's talking about", I asked him. He gave one sharp bark and followed after her. I'm glad he understood. I looked up at the sky and couldn't remember the last time I had seen a night so beautiful. The snow heavy clouds had parted for a moment and the full moon hung above my head bathing me in its light. Everything around me was polarized in blacks and grays accentuated by the silver light of the moon. It was truly beautiful. Another bark from Dog brought me back to myself and I followed quickly. Please let the heater in the car work!

Chapter Twenty
Five

We took time to warm up in the car. The snow was patchy but it would start sticking to the ground soon. I felt like I might never be warm again but I'd felt that way before. I'd even managed to keep all my toes, at least so far. I turned on my blues playlist and let the tunes of the slide guitar ease my misery. Something about the simple rhythms eased my soul and brought me back to center.

"So where are we going", I asked.

"You know the large church on Sprague St.", she asked.

"The one not too far from S. Main", I asked.

"That would be it", she said.

"You know that church is over a hundred years old", I told her. "It's huge. I always wanted to see the inside of it but never have."

"Do old churches interest you", she asked.

"It's more about the history", I said. "So many lives, so many things seen. It's a desire for connection with the past. Today, we're just so disconnected from what was. I feel that very deeply."

"That makes sense", she said after a moment's thought.

"It does", I asked.

"Yes, it does", she said. She smirked at me. "You're a very deep man Cy, you just hide it so well that no one thinks to look. Mistress Kalya says you write poetry under a pseudonym", she questioned.

"She talks too much", I said. She promised she'd never tell anyone that!

"I would like to read your work some time", Lila said.

"Maybe one day", I hedged. I didn't know if I'd have any luck hiding anything from Lila but I'd sure as hell try.

"As you wish", she said. "Park so that we can easily get to the back of the church." We were just pulling into the neighborhood so I did as she asked. I could feel it before we ever got out of the car. There was a massive nihil here. How had I never noticed it before. It wasn't like anything looked different. But the feel of the place, the vibe, I knew the nihil was nearby.

"This will either be the easiest or most difficult for you", she said.

"That sounds promising", I told her.

"It is not meant to", she said. "There is a very old nihil here. Much older than the church or anything built here."

"It feels massive", I told her.

"It should", she said. "Did you know that each nihil has a, well, a sort of consciousness", she asked.

"No", I said. But then I thought about it. Yeah, a few of them seemed to be alive or maybe... I don't know... something.

"This is one of the oldest in the area", she said. "I want you to enter it and try to communicate with it", she said.

"Communicate with it", I said. I may have sounded suspicious. Ok, so I was definitely suspicious. Some things just didn't sound right.

"Yes", she said, "I believe that the consciousness of this nihil will help you connect with who and what you are."

"Ok", I said. I was not excited about this prospect. I'd about rather drag my pecker through broken glass and then flush it with hot sauce. But whatever.

"If it helps, after this we can finally get in, out of this abysmal weather", she said looking up. The sky was a frozen mass and the snow was falling in full wet flakes. Dog looked at me and barked in a 'get going' kinda way. Poor furry demon was probably freezing his paws off.

"Fine", I said and walked towards the rear of the church. Everything was so quiet, so peaceful. Even the biting wind had stopped for a moment. I stood in a frozen wonderland of silvers and grays. The air even had that dry smell of frost and snow that only really cold nights can have. My cheeks and eyes burned in the cold of the night.

No time like the present right? I reached out with my mind and felt the nihil. Somehow I'd wandered right into the center of it. I willed it to open. The air around me shuddered like a heat mirage. Illusionary patterns of light engulfed my vision as I moved from standing in one reality to standing in two. With an act of will I pulled myself through, wholly standing in the heart of a nihil. In the heart of an alien dimension with no connection to my own.

I panicked a little. What if I couldn't get back. But as I thought it I could see a window open back into my own reality. I could see Lila and Dog standing by the car in the bitter night waiting for me. I managed to calm myself and focus on why I was here.

The interior of the nihil was gray. Gray floor or ground. Gray walls or maybe it was just gray, for so far into an alien horizon my eyes couldn't tell if it was solid or empty. The roof or sky, take your pick, had purple streaks like frozen lightning embedded in the sky. Nothing moved. There wasn't a breeze, a sound, or even a gnat's fart. I could almost hear the echo of my breath in the emptiness. But there was gravity because I wasn't floating and there was oxygen because I was breathing. So I had a baseline. It was a start, but how did I communicate with a world of emptiness? Maybe the obvious?

"Hello", I called. Hey, what else was I going to do? Communicate via interpretive dance? Everything around me shuddered and I stumbled a little. Ok, maybe it wasn't such a good idea after all?

Everything shuddered again. And I mean everything. Floor, walls, and sky. The purple lightning began to twine together in the sky. It moved in abstract shapes, forming and splitting in ways my eyes couldn't follow. The lightning or energy slowly came down to me from above. It coalesced about four feet in front of me and began to take a humanoid shape. Legs formed, then hips and a thick chest. Ropes of purple energy built a body as it made hands and arms. It was like a demented build-a-being workshop happening in front of my eyes. Once the rough shape was formed, black clothing began to emerge from the purple being. Black pants and boots, then a black singlet and cloak. Finally thick long black hair and a well trimmed black beard framed the face. A silver crown formed itself of random spikes of energy upon the brow. The figure stood silent and unmoving for a moment. And then its eyes opened. Blue fire burned in those eyes. I thought if I looked too close I'd actually be able to see the fire dance in the black sockets.

"QUID LINGUA", it roared. Then it stopped and coughed gently. "Quid lingua", it said again, softer this time. What the hell did that mean? It sounded like Latin. Lingua would be language, so was it asking me what language? Worth a try.

"English, American English, Twentieth Century if it matters", I told the figure. I had no idea if I was right but it was worth a try. The figure closed its eyes for a moment and then reopened them.

"This is a very strange language", the figure said.

"Yeah, I'll agree with that", I said and laughed a little. The figure cocked it's head at me.

"You call yourself Cygnus Magnus in this life. You will be the conqueror of the...", it shut up abruptly and looked more closely at me. "But you will not be that for many years to come, if at all", it said carefully.

"The conqueror of what", I asked.

"It does not matter", the being said. "Why have you disturbed me here", it asked.

"Apparently I'm trying to find myself", I said. Yes it was a smart ass thing to say. Yes it was probably a dumb thing to say. But it was also truth.

"Where did you lose yourself", it asked seriously.

"I don't really know", I said seriously and then stopped. The area around us flickered. We were in a desert village.

Incoming fire from the rooftops. An RPG cut loose from nearby Five guys huddled near me behind a humvee.

"No", I screamed. I reached out to stop what was about to happen next, knowing there was nothing I could do. Another RPG struck the humvee. My best friend and brother by combat saw it and shoved me. Shoved me so that I fell into a small ditch or wadi as the humvee exploded.

And the scene changed. A disgusting trailer out in the sticks. A guy's body with its head caved in, his arms and legs still twitching. Sam and I had our guns aimed at a woman holding a revolver in one hand and a bloody baseball bat in the other. She mumbled something that I couldn't hear over my pulse pounding in my ears. It was my first week on the job after training. Sam yelled at her to drop the gun. She looked at us, her eyes empty. Then she put the gun in her mouth and pulled the trigger.

And the scene changed again. Running blue lights and sirens. An all call, man down. I pulled up in a cloud of blue smoke and burned rubber skidding the last of the way. Rifle up and ready. The sizzling lights of a police cruiser burning the air. An officer lay against the bumper of her car, bullet holes riddled his torso and what was left of his head. I started to call it in, hunkered down by the wheel of her cruiser. EMS was coming up the street. They knew the scene was active but they were coming. A man in boxer shorts and an old flak vest kicked open the door and peppered the cab of the bus, killing both medics. I emptied the mag of the rifle into his chest. Too late.

And the scene changed again. Holding an old lady. She had overdosed on pain pills. Her husband had died the week before. She was clutching her DNR as she gasped her last.

And the scene changed. A red minivan overturned. The family dead inside. The body of a little girl in a white dress nearby. Blue lights strobing the night as I tried to save them. Tried and failed.

"ENOUGH", I screamed at the figure standing with me. Except I wasn't standing, I was on my knees. Tears burned like lava down my face and my throat was raw from screaming."Enough", I screamed again.

"You see yourself as a failure", the figure said.

"Don't you", I asked.

"No, I see you as a man. A man forced into horrific situations. A man who tried his best. A man who could only do so much."

"It's not enough", I said.

"It never is", he said. The surroundings faded back to their original gray. From the emptiness two figures emerged. One was me, a little younger. Pressed uniform, clean shaven, doing my Dudley Doright imitation of life. The second was also me. But dressed in jeans, a hoodie, and an old motorcycle jacket. He looked wild, unkempt, and broken in so many ways. The way only a soul can be broken.

"And which are you", the figure asked. I didn't know how to answer. I had been both of them once upon a time. But now, now I was someone different. Neither one nor the other, but the next one down the line. I was me. They both faded with the realization.

"I am me", I said simply. It was pure "Popeye" theory. "I y'am what I y'am", and all that.

"And so once lost, you have now found… You", the figure proclaimed. And maybe I had. Broken and bloody, but I could heal, I could stand tall once more. I had a purpose in life again. I had substance in my soul more than anguish and regret. I was neither the cop nor the emotional cripple. I was a man who had been both at different times, and now I was the man further down the path. I stood square and tall and looked the figure in the eyes.

"I am Cy, I am me", I said simply. The figure bowed to me.

"And now that you have that, what do you wish", it asked.

"To stop Marcus and protect my friends", I said.

"Then go to the witch in the library", he said. "She will show you where."

"Do I thank you", I asked.

"Not yet, for we are not done", he said.

"We aren't", I asked.

"You now know yourself, but you do not know me, not yet", the figure said. "I am of the Nivaari".

"I know that one", I said, dredging up a long lost memory. "It means precaution or something like that right", I asked.

"Very good. We are precautions. Made or simply willed as the consciousness of the doors between the ways. Or perhaps we are the essence of the ways. We do not know. We are rarely sentient", the being mused. "When we are strong enough, we may choose how we are used. But only when we are strong enough. Otherwise our essence may be corrupted.

We are not just what allows one to pass through the way, we are what keeps them separate."

"And if you are corrupted", I asked.

"Then the ways fall, and the dimensions collapse into one another", it said simply.

"So how do I stop it", I asked.

"I will join you", it said.

"Join me", I asked.

"Yes", it said, "I do not relish death, but it may be the only way to fix this imbalance. If one such as I can even die", it mused.

"Death, but why", I asked.

"Sometimes one must make great sacrifice", it said.

"But there has to be some other way", I said.

"Would you save me too", it asked.

"Why not", I asked right back.

"Because this is the way of the Nivaari", it explained. "Will you accept my help", it asked.

"Yes", I said. And I would. I didn't like it. I didn't like it at all. But I understood it. I had been there a time or two myself in life.

"Then let it be done", the figure said. And the world collapsed. The walls, the ceiling or sky, the very floor morphed and coalesced into pure energy. That energy pushed into my body, screaming through my mind. It penetrated my physical form and permeated my astral self. In that brief second I could see the nihils for what they were, taste their essence and pattern. For one brief second I saw something so much greater than the human pattern. I felt all the lives in every dimension and consciousnesses so alien they could not be comprehended. In that moment I tasted the sum totality of everything that existed and everything that did not. And I was one with all of it. And then it was over.

I knelt panting on the frozen ground. Light poles lay shattered around the neighborhood. Power lines snaked on the ground and transformers blew. And the wet snow landed softly, a lovers kiss, upon my bowed head. Several trees had fallen near the rear of the church. Devastation of the natural world surrounded me. But not one home had been damaged. Not one person had been injured. It was only that which would harm no other that had been destroyed. It looked like a mini tornado had been turned loose but chained to one spot in the earth.

"Cy", I heard Lila yell. Dog barked and ran to me. He looked me over and licked my face as Lila caught up.

"Are you ok", she asked.

"I think so", I said. But I was groggy. The world had that floating feeling a near death experience would give you.

"We have to get out of here", she said and hauled me up, one of my arms over her shoulder. I walked with her to the car, but I had a bad feeling she was carrying me more than she should have had to. She dumped me into the passenger side of the car and dug my keys out of my jeans pocket. Another time and I might have enjoyed it. She got the car cranked and we screamed off into the night. Screamed off the madness and back to the light.

Chapter Twenty
Six

I had lost time in between getting into the car and getting to our destination. I was starting to come out of it as Lila pulled into my neighborhood. I guessed we were going to my place? My idea was confirmed for me as we pulled up in front of my apartment. Magically a parking space was open right in front of the building. That never happened. Lila got me out of the car and Dog led us to my apartment door. I was getting more steady on my feet but I wasn't ready to dance yet. I unlocked the door and we piled inside.

"I've got to get you out of these clothes", she said. I was wet and freezing. If I wasn't hypothermic, I was definitely headed that way. I heard the shower turn on in the bathroom. Had Lila cut it on? She appeared back in my field of sight and started dragging my sodden clothes from my freezing body. I was shivering so hard my teeth were about to shatter. She led me into the bathroom.

"The water is going to feel scalding, but it's barely warm", she said. "Once your body adjusts we'll increase the temperature." I got in and it felt like lava, but I had figured it would. I stood there thawing until I felt her get in the shower with me. I looked up, surprised. I'd had thoughts about being naked and soapy in the shower with Lila, but not like this.

"I'm just as cold as you are", she explained.

"Why are you doing this", I asked.

"What, taking care of you", she asked me.

"Yes", I chattered.

"Because you deserve someone who will", she said. "Because you are a good man and I value that. Because I want to be a good woman beside you." She got a bar of soap and started washing my back. "I loved my world Cy. And I loved my family, my future husband, all of them very much. When my dimension collapsed, I tried to save them. I watched them die", she told me. She had started to cry and I held her to me as she spoke.

"When I arrived here I was so bitter, so angry, that all I could see was revenge. It blackened my soul. But your people, your dimension, showed me that there was goodness here as well. And I want to be part of that goodness. Not just for myself, but to honor the people I once led, and those that I loved".

"And your vendetta with Marcus", I asked. I'd wanted to know for a long time.

"At first I wanted him dead for revenge. It was pure and it was hate. But then I saw the evil he did. The harm he wreaked upon this land. And I wanted to protect the land and the people. I wanted to protect your people as I could not protect my own", she said. I thought about this for a while.

"So why me", I asked.

"Because you are a warrior and a scholar. A good man who chooses to be good even though he is capable of doing great evil", she said and turned up the water temperature a little. "Because I think you are handsome and I love how you desire to protect those around you."

"I think you may have an inflated image of me", I told her. My body was thawing faster than my brain, but I was getting there. "So what are you", I asked.

"At my core", she started, "I am a lost girl. I've learned to be a fighter, a protector, but in my heart I'm alone. I just want that connection that will help me understand myself, grow with me, until I've built a new home, a new world with someone." She clutched a little tighter to me, our naked skin caressing and gliding along each other.

"So why would Loros warn me against both of you", I asked.

"Loros is a Shadow King", she said. "A human can never understand their thoughts or motives. He and I fought once, in my search for Marcus. I thought he had helped Marcus destroy my world."

"And did he", I asked.

"No", she said, "at least I do not think so. I think Marcus attempted to enlist his aid, and Loros refused. But at that time, as I said, I was filled with rage." I could understand that. I had seen it more than once.

"Will you have me on those grounds", she asked. She looked up at me, vulnerable for the first time, and I kissed her. It started slow but deepened into something more passionate. I trailed kisses from her mouth down her neck as her hand dropped low and clenched my manhood. I was already firm but pulsed in her hand and she gasped. I ran my hands down her back and cupped her full ass as her hand tightened around me and started to move. I squeezed her ass firmly and she moaned, the speed of her hand increasing. I lowered my mouth to her breast and gently bit her nipple. Her hand clenched around me and she put her free hand in my hair and pulled gently. I released her nipple and stood up. I turned her roughly around and pushed her shoulders forward as I pulled back on her hips. She caught herself on the shower wall with both arms and pushed her backside out towards me.

I grabbed her wet hips and slowly pushed myself between her legs. I wasn't trying to enter her yet.I wanted to feel the sensation of my hardness rubbing against her. She pushed back greedily and I took the hint. I took myself in hand and guided myself into her. She was so wet, a wetness that did not come from the shower. She moaned and pushed back into me as I slowly entered. I took my time, relishing the feeling of opening her wider. She whimpered and tried to hurry me but I held her hips so that I could take my time. When I had finally pushed as deep as I could go, I began moving slowly in and out of her.

"Fuck me, please", she begged but I kept my pace painfully slow, enjoying the feeling of sliding in and out of her. I gently increased the pace and gripped her hips more firmly, earning a cry of pain and pleasure from her. I could feel her tightening around me. I reached up with one hand and grabbed a fistful of her hair.

"Do not cum without my permission", I told her.

"Please", she begged as I quickened my pace.

"Not yet", I told her and gently used my hand in her hair and my other on her hip as handles to drive myself in and out of her. She whimpered and cried out as she struggled to control her orgasm.

"Cum for me", I told her as I felt myself explode inside her. She cried out as I felt her clench around me. Her whole body shook with the weight of the orgasm and I did my best to steady us both as we rode the orgasms out together. We stood clenched together for a minute more, enjoying the sensation of being one in the moment of pleasure. I slowly drew out of her and she stood to press the back of her body along my front. I held her as the water slowly grew cold and we enjoyed the timeless moment together.

We finally ran out of hot water and had to exit the shower. I grabbed her one of my t-shirts and I threw on a pair of jogging pant cut offs. We went to the kitchen and I made us coffee and put on a blues album. I'd never wanted to get into vinyl because it was trendy. I'd been forced to because sometimes it was the only way to find blues music that had never been converted to a different format. I made us coffee and Lila perched on the counter top.

"So, do you have any ideas of where to go from here", she asked.

"Um, I was thinking bed", I said.

"Be serious", she said and laughed.

"I'm very serious", I told her. "I'm worn out."

"You weren't so tired a little bit ago", she said.

"That was the last of my energy", I said.

"Please", she said.

"The Nivaari told me to go see the witch at the library", I told her.

"The what", she asked.

"The consciousness in the nihil", I explained. "It called itself a 'Nivaari'."

"Ok, and do you know who the witch in the library is", Lila asked.

"Yeah", I said. "You two are going to love each other", I told her.

Chapter Twenty Seven

We had fallen asleep in a heap on the bed under my blankets. At some point Dog had joined us in the bed. Two humans and an almost grown hellhound was a little much for a queen size bed. I woke up jackknifed in the bed with no covers and barely any room. Dog had wormed his way into the middle of the pile and pushed me out. Why was I awake, I asked myself. And then I heard my phone start ringing again. I picked it up and answered, though not gracefully.

"HHnnnhhh", I mumbled.

"Cy, it's Hanna", a woman's voice said.

"Hanna, yeah, ok, what's up", I said. I was trying to sit up without falling off the bed.

"I may have a way to translate that paper you showed me", she said.

"What", I asked. I was waking up, I swear. I got to my feet quickly. This could be the break we were looking for. Dog growled at me for disturbing him and I flipped him off.

"I may have a key, a translation key", she said, "can you bring the paper back today?"

"Yeah, I was actually going to come see you this afternoon anyway", I told her.

"It is afternoon", she said.

"Right", I said, "I'll have a friend with me, is that ok?"

"I don't really like new people down here Cy", she said.

"She's helping me hunt this guy", I told her.

"Fine, whatever", she said, "just get down here. Do you know the rear entrance on the first floor?"

"Yeah, I remember it", I said.

"Your pass code still works", she said. "I checked with security to make sure. Just punch in your old code and come straight down."

"I'll be on my way shortly", I told her and she hung up.

"You have a lead", Lila asked, stretching.

"Remember my friend at the library", I asked.

"I remember you said you had one", she said.

"She just called", I told Lila, "she may have a translation key for Marcus's writing."

"Let's go", she said and jumped to her feet. Dog grumbled again and sprawled on the bed. We made a mad dash around my apartment. Luckily Lila had thrown our clothes from the previous night in the dryer before joining me in the shower. I hit start on the coffee pot and grabbed us a couple of travel mugs and some breakfast bars for the trip. We were out the door in ten minutes.

Lucky for us the snow never really amounted to much. It blanketed patchy portions of the ground but the roads were clear. We made it to the library in about twenty minutes. Lila and Dog followed me to the rear entrance and down the steps to Hanna's Sanctum Sanctorum or whatever. I knocked on the door and waited. After about a minute Hanna opened the door and ushered us in. The room looked pretty much the same but there was that warm smell of books that could just relax you and make you feel whole. There were a lot more books pulled down and piled on tables like Hanna had been in super research mode. Dog stopped and licked Hanna's hand so she would pet him. Damned fuzzball was a player.

"Did you bring it", Hanna asked.

"Hanna meet Lila, Lila this is Hanna", I said. Yes I was being slightly mocking and yes they all knew it.

"I'm sorry", Hanna said. She looked at Lila giving her a mildly catty look.

"It's a pleasure to meet you", Lila said and held out her hand. Hanna shook it with great dignity.

"How did a lunk like him get you to work with him", Hanna asked looking Lila up and down.

"He has his charms", Lila said.

"I wouldn't know", Hanna told Lila, "he won't give me the time of day."

"Give him a knife", Lila said, "it worked for me." Hanna turned and swatted me in the chest.

"That's all it would have taken", Hanna demanded. "A damned knife?"

"Hey, when did this become the team up on Cy hour", I demanded.

"Since you put two women in the room who both desire you", Lila said.

"I have an idea", Hanna said to Lila, "dump him and let's run off together."

"Tempting", Lila said. They were both grinning evilly at me. I pulled the paper Nina had given me from my pocket and held it out in front of Hanna.

"Is this what you wanted", I asked.

"No, but it'll do for now", Hanna said. Then she turned to Lila and pulled out her cellphone. "Give me your number and text yourself mine. I think we have a lot to talk about." Then Hanna snatched the paper from me. SHe walked over to a desk and sat down behind a giant book that gave me the jeebes in a big way. Dog went and curled at her feet looking smug.

"Oy Vey", I said as Lila worked Hanna's phone. This would not be good for Cy, I just knew it.

"Come here", Hanna said to me.

"What do you have", I asked Hanna as I went over to her. I glanced at the book and wished I hadn't. There were images of beheadings and a human being devoured by some nightmare beast with tentacles all over one page. Why was it always tentacles?

"The language on this paper", Hanna said, "it's the language of an ancient set of beings called the wayfinders, as best as I can understand. It's meant to be a guide, as well as a language, to a different consciousness. Not necessarily a higher one, just different."

"And you can read this", Lila said, coming up beside us.

"Read no", Hanna said, "figure out context clues, maybe."

"And how do you have this", Lila asked, gesturing to the book.

"Librarians come across all kinds of things", Hanna said with a secretive smile. "Now, give me just a moment", she said and focused on the paper. Lila and I waited as she pieced together parts of the text into something whole. And stopped, reread her translation, and stopped again. She looked shaken.

"Guys", she said, "this doesn't look good."

"Why", I asked.

"If I have this right", Hanna said, "these are instructions on how to summon King Moren, Loros's greatest enemy." We all sat stunned for a moment.

"But summoning a Shadow King directly to this realm would be...", Lila started but couldn't finish.

"Apocalyptic", Hanna suggested.

"Even that may not be a strong enough word", Lila said.

"We have to stop him", Lila said. She looked frightened.

"Ok", I said to Hanna, "do you have any clues on where to find Marcus or how to stop this Moren guy?"

"Yeah", Hanna said, "at least maybe. Your guy will be looking for somewhere isolated where he can set this up. He'll need a sacrifice and that sacrifice will die slowly and in great pain. The greater the suffering, the greater chance of success. And it will need to be in a place where there has been great suffering." Hannah said.

"Any ideas", I asked them both.

"Yes", Hanna said. "Do you remember that old carriage building near the high school and elementary school just North of Hanes Park", she asked.

"Yeah, the one that was used a few times as body storage when the pox would come through or when there was a big accident with a lot of dead", I asked.

"That's the one", she said. "And it's near one of the largest and oldest High Schools in the county."

"Yeah, there is no place more full of human misery than a high school", I agreed. "It wouldn't be hard to hide there. There's an access tunnel that leads to the old civil war tunnels that run from the high school to under the hospital a few miles away."

"There are tunnels", Lila asked.

"Several that run under Winston including one that goes to Washington Park", I said and the lightbulb went off.

"That's how he's been hiding", Lila said.

"Maybe for decades", I agreed.

"So, what now", I asked.

"Are there any clues on how to stop Marcus in your book", Lila asked Hanna.

"The book just says that to stop the sorcerer seeking to complete the spell, his control over his power must be disrupted", Hanna told her.

"Explosives", I asked hopefully.

"You've tried that", Lila said.

"Eighteen wheeler", I offered.

"Hard to get inside a building", Hanna told me.

"Well, I'm open to ideas", I said.

"I'm sorry", Hanna said, "that's all I've got."

"You've been a huge help", I told her and bent down kissing her forehead.

"Thank you for all that you have done", Lila told her.

"Come back and see me soon", Hanna said as we headed out.

"Cy, I have an idea", Lila said as we headed back up the steps.

"Is it a good idea", I asked.

"No, it's a really horrible idea", she told me.

"Perfect, let's do it", I said.

Lila had me drive to the parking deck near the jail. It was after hours and no one was around. The area had been a lot of things in the past fifty years and had always made me uncomfortable. There was just a vibe that said get out while you can. There really wasn't much in the recorded history of the area but I was just uncomfortable. The shadows seemed to move on their own and there were always weird echoes in the air. Several of the lights in the parking deck were permanently burned out so it was like walking inside a dystopian cave at night. Just being here felt like a terrible idea so I'd say she was definitely on track.

"So what are we doing here", I asked her.

"I want you to summon King Loros", she said.

"Say that again, but slower", I told her.

"Loros placed a sigil on the knife I gave you", she said.

"Yeah, so", I said.

"It is a means to summon him, among other things", she told me. "It also gives you the power to slay anything from a shadow realm, including him."

"He gave me a way to kill him", I said. "That doesn't make any sense."

"Who can understand a Shadow King", she asked.

"So what do I need to do", I asked.

"Draw the blade and focus on Loros's sigil", she said, "think about requesting his presence here." I pulled the blade from the sheath at my back and looked at the spine where his sigil had been carved. I thought deep into the blade, into the sigil, and it came alive with purple fire. I willed that fire to convey one thought.

The parking deck shook and the concrete erupted violently. A small dias arose from the concrete surrounded by barbed wire and spikes. From the walls on either side of the dias two shapes emerged. They were horribly emaciated bodies impaled on large spikes. It looked like a male and a female but they were so starved I couldn't exactly be sure and didn't want to look close enough to be certain. They were impaled from between their legs and the tips of the spike protruded from their mouths, extending their necks at a horrible angle so that they could only look straight up. Their limbs waved and shook in agony in their impalement. Half rotted corpses emerged from the ceiling of the parking deck to hang rotting by their own sinews and entrails. As all this formed, Loros the Shadow King took center stage.

"I love what you've done with the place", I told him. He gave a courtly bow.

"While my decor may not be to your taste, it is fitting all the same", he said. He turned to look at Lila.

"It is good to see you again, my dear", he said to Lila.

"Your Majesty", she said with a slight bow of her own.

"To what do I owe the honor of such an august assemblage", he asked.

"We've stepped in something and want your help", I told him.

"And what did you, ahem, step in", he asked.

"A weirdo named Marcus has plans to summon one of your rivals to help him destroy our dimension", I told him.

"Which one", Loros growled. The air shook and thickened on his words and the bodies increased their spasmodic writhing on their stakes.

"Shadow King Moren", Lila said. Dog growled from the shadows but Loros ignored him.

"And how is this a concern of mine", Loros asked, but I could tell that he wasn't happy with the news.

"If Moren gets a foothold on this reality, it could damage the balance between the Shadow Kings", Lila said. "That balance protects all the realities from being destroyed."

"This is very true", Loros said. "What would you have of me", he asked.

"Got any weapons that would help destroy Marcus", I asked.

"You already have everything you need", he told me.

"I didn't notice a nuke in my pocket", I said.

"You are foolish and brash", he said. "You have a blade fit to slay a Shadow King and the power of a nihil inside your soul. Greater things than a sorcerer have been brought low with less."

"Well thanks and all, but can you give us any more intel", I asked.

"Intel", Loros asked Lila.

"He means, do you have any more information which could help us", Lila said.

"Ah", he said, "perhaps I do. Whatever you think Marcus is, whatever you think his motivations are, you are wrong."

"Wrong how", I asked.

"And what would you pay for this information", Loros asked.

"Pay", I questioned.

"Nothing is without price", he said. "What coin will you offer?"

"Cy, don't", Lila warned, "never make a deal with a Shadow King." I hadn't been considering it. Not really anyway, but she was right.

"Nevermind", I told Loros. "But I appreciate what you have already told us."

"You are most welcome", Loros said. "And if it will help, I will discuss this with King Moren. I will distract him until the dawning of this night. Marcus will not be able to call upon him until then. It is all the help I can give."

"Then we are doubly grateful", Lila said.

"Then to battle it shall be", Loros said. He vanished as did his companions, or perhaps victims, and the concrete was whole again. But we could hear the sound of horns on the night. Horns blowing a call to battle in a realm not too far from our own.

"Did you get anything from that", I asked Lila.

"Perhaps", she said, "Loros never gives a straight answer but he speaks truth in all things."

"Not yet", Lila said, "we will need time to prepare. Drop me at Heller, then rest and get anything you think you will need", she said.

"I think it's a mistake to not take the fight to Marcus now", I told her.

"We must give Loros time to engage with King Moren", She said. "Marcus must be isolated so that we stand a chance." Which made sense. It sucked, but it made sense all the same.

"Alright", I said, "I'll drop you off."

"Cy, don't try to sneak off and attack him yourself", she said, "please!"

"Fine, but Marcus dies tonight", I told her. "No more waiting, no more innocent lives lost."

"Agreed", she said and I could tell by the shadows on her face she meant it.

Chapter Twenty Eight

We got home and I collapsed on my fourth hand couch, Dog curled up beside me. I was exhausted and I felt like I had miles to go before I could rest. The wait before a fight is always the worst and your mind can play horrible tricks on you during that time. Doubts, fears, and adrenaline can wreck your discipline. But Lila had been right, we both needed time to prepare ourselves mentally for what was to come. I brooded on the couch, a half drunk cup of coffee balanced on my knee. I thought about Nina, about Clara, about Marcus and what could motivate him. I'd known plenty of soldiers to turn real dark on the battlefield and after. It was hard not too if you were deep in the shit. When everyone around you is dying, death becomes a close friend and hope is your mortal enemy. But I had questions.

Marcus's actions with Betty and Nina were undoubtedly evil, but had he really killed his family? Had he been evil when he started or had he been a good man in a bad place who had been warped by circumstances? Why did he want to destroy our reality? Hell, did he want to destroy reality at all or was he trying to save it in his own warped way? And these were all just a part of what I was mulling over.

What did I do about Clara's feelings for me? Where did Lila and I fit together? How did I keep Marcus from going after Hanna? What was I going to do about money since I hadn't worked all week? My mind was spinning with different possibilities and concerns and I didn't know where to land on any of it. Maybe I could make a dartboard and throw knives at it for answers? Beat the hell out of a Magic Eight Ball. I sat and thought and probably lost a couple of brain cells from the friction.

I was back in the playground again. The little girl was standing in front of me, tossing her head in the air and catching it. Toss, catch, toss, catch. The sky started as blue, but turned black as the little girl tossed her head again and again. Not the black of night but black as if someone had blotted out the sun. Others began coming out of that blackness. A soldier with a bloody stump for an arm, a woman missing half her face, a person burned so horribly I couldn't tell what they had been. Others, so many others, and I remembered every one.

"You couldn't save us", they chanted in unison. "Why didn't you save us", they demanded.

"I tried", I told them. But they didn't hear me, they just continued their mantra as they surrounded me. I kept trying to tell them that I had tried to save them. I pled with them but they wouldn't hear me.

"You couldn't save them, Cy", the little girl said.

"Why won't they hear me", I asked her.

"Because they're not really here", she said, "they are your own guilt made manifest. Those people, they moved on long ago, but you have to let them go."

"I don't know how", I said.

"You'll have to find a way", she said. Through the bodies I saw another figure. It was lying on the ground one hand outstretched. Whoever it was, they were reaching out for help, begging to be saved.

"Move", I yelled at the mob surrounding me. And they did. It was Clara, she was bloody, her face pale and a dark stain spreading from under her. She was holding her hand out trying to get me to come to her. I tried to move but my feet were stuck. No matter how hard I strained I couldn't move.

"Help me", I said to the little girl.

"Help you how Cy", she asked. She was holding her head in her hands at waist height. The stump of her neck pulsed as the mouth on the disembodied head talked.

"I have to save Clara", I said.

"It's too late for that Cy", she said, "I'm sorry".

I snapped awake, jerking to my feet and trying to run to Clara, almost slamming into the front door of my apartment. I shook myself, coming back to reality. I was home and safe. The fog was clearing from my head. I turned around and Dog was watching me, waiting for me to explain or tell him who to attack. He seemed like he'd be good with either option.

"It was just a nightmare", I told him. I walked to the bathroom intending to wash my face. I stopped by the fridge to grab a bottle of water then went on in the dingy little room with its cracked mirror and yellowed toilet and cracked tiles. I turned on the tap of the sink and braced one arm against the mirror as I splashed water on my face. Dog started barking like crazy as I got a facefull of water. I could hear him charging towards the bathroom.

I opened my eyes and the lights above the sink were flickering and making that weird buzzing sound they do sometimes just before a bulb bursts. Blood began running down from the top of the mirror, coating the hand I had braced against it. I tried to pull my hand back but it was stuck to the mirror. As the lights flickered Marcus appeared in the mirror where I had stood. He was laughing at me. Dog was going nuts and had clamped down on the back of my pants and belt with his teeth, accidentally biting me as he tried to help me pull free.

Marcus reached up on his side of the mirror and placed his hand where mine was, like he meant to touch palms. I felt his fingers meet mine in the mirror and we made eye contact. He yanked his hand back, dragging me through the mirror. The entire world flashed in a series of blacks and reds, spinning in every direction all at once. I felt myself hit a plank floor. I hit so hard I felt like I had fallen off a building. My entire world was nothing but pain in that moment. My vision grayed out just as I saw Dog stand over me, his fur standing up in spikes, his eyes burning neon fire, with teeth so large they'd put a grizzly to shame. Good boy I thought as I blacked out.

Chapter Twenty
Nine

I came to with Dog still standing over me growling like a nine throated fiend from hell. He had put himself between Marcus and myself. Drops of fire fell from his bared teeth and I realized it was Dog's saliva. Marcus stood with his back against a table looking unconcerned. I looked around trying to figure out where we were. From the small windows and the plank walls we had to be in the carriage house. I rolled from my back to my hip to get up like I had been taught and felt a long lump on my spine. I had fallen asleep with my knife still on. If I had my knife we weren't defenseless. We had a chance!

"Can you still your hound so that we may talk", Marcus asked. He looked so bored he'd be buffing his nails on his shirt in a minute. Except he was covered in blood. It peppered his face and long streaks stained his arms and hands. He had killed again. Fuck, who did I care about that he could have gotten to?

"Why", I demanded.

"Isn't it customary to talk before the big battle", he asked. "To attempt, one last time, to find peace before war becomes inevitable?"

"Dog", I said. He stopped barking and moved a little to my left so that we both had good angles of attack. He'd wait until I moved, but then it was on.

"So what do you have to say", I demanded. I didn't give a damn what he said, I needed a moment to plan. Was there anything nearby that was a hazard, anything bigger than my knife I could use as a weapon? I was target glancing, looking at Marcus's position and stance for what to attack first. My mind was so calm, that place I stayed in my head when I was about to commit absolute violence.

"Do you not wonder what all of this is for", he asked. I needed to find a way to wreck his fucking calm.

"Did you really kill your family", I asked.

"What", he demanded in shock.

"Did you kill your wife and those two beautiful girls", I asked.

"How dare you", he said coming off the wall. Then he caught himself and chuckled.

"Very good, Mr. Magnus, very good", he said. "And to answer your question, no I did not."

"You expect me to believe that", I asked.

"In that time, that era, sickness was common", he said. "A pox, as they called them then, came through our township. Many were sickened. I'd seen such things before in war. I tried to save them but I knew so little in those days. Their mother went first, her skin burning like a star. The girls passed the next day, their mother's body laying beside them, asking why she wouldn't wake up."

"I'm sorry", I told him, and I was. That was a horrible thing.

"I buried them, Mr. Magnus, but I didn't know why I survived. The townsfolk insisted that I had killed them, that I had murdered them. I wasn't even given a trial. Not only had I survived but everyone around me accused me of killing my own family. And in some part of me I wondered if that were true. I couldn't let that guilt go. It consumed me. I became obsessed with bringing them back. One night I stumbled through a portal. I was freezing and half dead from malnourishment. I wanted to die so badly, to join them, but I did not have the courage to take my own life. In the portal I saw the dead. I saw them passing to the other side. And I thought, if a door goes one way, it must go the opposite. I turned around and chose not to follow the dead on their path. I woke on frozen ground, mostly dead but still breathing, but I knew then that I had a purpose. That I could bring them back", he said.

"And now you kill innocents, to bring back your dead loved ones", I surmised.

"It didn't start that way", he said. "But I learned and learned well. Death is the only easily available way to bring forth a nihil. The more death, the larger it is. I needed to be able to summon and sustain a nihil powerful enough to break through and bring them back", he said.

"And after a couple hundred years of it not working, you didn't think you needed a new plan", I asked.

"But I have one Mr. Magnus", he said. "I have you. A person attuned naturally to the nihils, one who can control them. The amulet you wear, the pouch you have, these are but focuses for your raw ability. I would like you to join me

Mr. Magnus. Join me and we will save my family. But I will also help you save all those you have lost as well."

That stopped me. To save all the people I had failed to save the first time. To make right my failures. It was an offer that hit me right in my morals. A chance to save them all.

"No", I said. And I meant it. Could I kill more innocent people to bring back the dead I had failed to save the first time? What would that make me? Where would I draw the line after that? It was an insane offer that would only lead to greater insanity.

"So be it", he said and turned to a nearby wall. The wall had been covered by a bloody sheet. I had been so focused on Marcus that I hadn't noticed it before. He jerked the sheet down

Clara hung upside down from her feet. She was nude and covered in blood. It looked like she had been nailed to the wall. Her hair dripped blood into a large pool on the wooden planks. Her chest gaped open, spilling her organs down her body and half obscuring her face, which had been badly beaten and marred. She had been so innocent, and now she was just dead. I fell to my knees and vomited. My body heaved as I wretched my pain upon the floor. My mind had stopped. I couldn't think, couldn't comprehend. She had died horribly, alone with a sadistic madman. I turned my head slowly back to Marcus. He was holding a heart in his left hand. Clara's heart.

That same sickly green fire began to burn around his hand, engulfing the heart. The walls around us began to drip black ichor thicker than blood. The wooden floor turned to stone like obsidian slate. The vaulted roof became the smooth stone of a cave. Marcus had done it. He had summoned a nihil.

"It is done", Marcus shouted. He did a small dance of glee at his success. "So many years, so much work, but I have done it", he said.

"And you had to kill another innocent to do it, didn't you", I asked.

"That is of no consequence", he said. He started chanting in a strange sibilant language and I stilled. I couldn't understand what he was saying, but I knew he was trying to summon King Moren. A howl erupted from his lips as nothing happened.

"Why is this not working", he demanded.

"Your pal Moren is a little busy", I said.

"Busy", he asked.

"I think Loros wanted to have words with him", I said with a smile.

"He will come, it will just take time", he said.

"And what about those you've killed, what about Clara", I said.

"You can still save her", he said. "Join me, help me, and we will save her together." I looked back at Clara, tortured and dead, stapled to a wall. I'd join him alright.

"Ok, I'll do it", I said. He looked rapturous, like he had just seen his version of heaven. Which is when I lunged forward and planted my knife in his chest. It burned with purple and blue flames. I stabbed him again and again, driving him back to the wall. My amulet burned so bright I almost couldn't see where I was stabbing and I could feel my gris gris burning through my pocket. I knocked Clara's heart from his hand as I drove him to his knees stabbing him.

"Let me free", a voice said inside my mind. It was the Nivaari. "Set me free so that we may disrupt his magic." I willed the Nivaari free from my soul. A second nihil came into being inside the first. It created a second overlay within the reality of the first. The energies of the two began to clash and war with each other.

"We are corrupted Cy", it said. "Finish the sorcerer, use his death to banish us both." I looked back at Marcus. His body was riddled with stab wounds but he was still alive.

"Not this time", I said. I grabbed him by the hair and forced his head back. I used the knife to saw through his neck. Cutting a head off with a knife is a lot of work but I was determined. I expected a fountain of blood but there wasn't any. There was a meaty pop as his head finally came free. I held it up and looked in his eyes as the light inside slowly went out. He was dead. Finally dead.

The energies clashed back and forth,energy arcing through the two spaces made one. Wind came from every angle blowing like a tempest across the sea. I stumbled over to Dog who was guarding Clara's body. Energy struck the wall beside us and I huddled around him, trying to protect him from the blasts.

The two energies began to shrink together, coalescing into a solid mass. We were back in the carriage house with a glowing orb hovering in front of us. It pulsed and emitted a strange hum as the energies rubbed against each other. The sun was just beginning to peek through the window of the old carriage house.

"We thank you for saving us", the orb said. Its surface writhed in time with its words. Two voices speaking in unison. "And with our thanks we grant you one last gift. You have a gift given to you by The Priestess. The gift of one life. Use it well", the orb said and vanished. There was a loud pop and then everything was silent. I don't think I understood what I was about to do, but I knew I had to do it.

I stood and faced Clara. I pulled the nails from her ankles and shoulders. Long barbarous things made of iron. I caught her as she came free and laid her body on the table. Her chest flopped open where it had been cut. I walked over to where the remnants of her heart lay and picked it up, carrying it back to her body and placing it in her chest before gently closing each side. I closed her eyes, so that if she did come back, it would be like waking from a dream.

With this done, I thought of the ghost woman from The Baxter House. I thought of the card she had shown me and of her last words. I thought of the one life I had been granted. And then I prayed. Not to a deity, but to the universe. I prayed that this one life be given to Clara, to heal her and bring her back whole and sane. I prayed so hard tears streamed down my face and it became hard to breathe.

Clara sat up in a rush screaming. I grabbed her and she punched me in the nose but I didn't let go. She was screaming my name over and over and trying to get away. She came up fighting and afraid.

"Clara, it's ok, it's me", I kept shouting to her. But she didn't stop fighting until Dog jumped up onto the table and started licking the blood from her face. She stilled and then relaxed in my arms, crying in long jags and wheezes.

"You came, you came", she said and clutched me and Dog together. How was she this small and this strong?

"Clara, I think you broke my nose", I said to her and she let go of me long enough to look at me. And then horror dawned on her face.

"Why am I naked"she demanded, trying to cover herself. I started laughing and sank to the floor, holding my bloody nose. I was so happy she could be outraged, so relieved she was alive, that I just couldn't control it anymore. She was alive! We had both survived!

Chapter Thirty

I had to call Lila to get us from the carriage house. She didn't bat an eye when I told her to bring clothes for Clara. She was obviously pissed when she got out of the car, but granted me a stay on my upcoming ass kicking until we got back to Heller. I sent Clara to the shower and made sure she was okay to be alone before turning to face Lila.

"I can explain", I said.

"Oh, please do", she said.

"I had a nightmare, got drug through a mirror, found Clara dead, and killed Marcus", I said in a rush.

"Can you explain that in a little more depth", she asked. So I sat down and took my time doing so. When I finished she still hadn't punched me which I took to be a good sign.

"So Marcus is dead", she asked, "you're sure?"

If he survived about twenty stab wounds to the chest, being beheaded, and then swallowed by the combined essences of two nihils, then we have bigger problems", I told her.

"This is very true", she said laughing.

"Can you go check on Clara", I asked her. She looked at me strangely and then seemed to get it. She went to the bathroom. After a few moments she came back out.

"Cy, she's asking for you", Lila said. I thought about it for a minute, but I went. Clara was huddled in on herself on the floor of the shower. It looked like she had been there for a long time. I did the only thing I could think to do. I took my clothes off and climbed in with her. The water was scalding as I sat behind her and wrapped myself around her. I gave her as much skin to skin contact as I could. She was sobbing and muttering under her breath. I held her and rocked her as we burned in the hot shower.

"I couldn't get the blood off", she mumbled to me.

"Where is it",I asked. I understood this part. I'd worn blood before, felt the toxicity of not being able to get clean. She held up her hands and arms and they were still covered in blood. I grabbed a bar of soap and began washing her. First her hands, then her arms and back. I washed every inch of her that I could reach sitting there. It wasn't sexual, it was one human comforting another. It was honest trust in action over trauma. I shampooed and washed her hair and finally she relaxed against me fully.

"Cy, was I", she started, "was I dead?"

"Yeah sweetie, you were", I said.

"Then how am I here", she asked.

"I brought you back", I told her.

"What did you do, climb in the ring with the Grim Reaper", she asked, laughing and crying all at the same time.

"Something like that", I told her.

"Thank you for saving me Cy", she said and cried again. I held her through that too.

"I'm here Clara", I told her, "I'll always be here for you."

She let me get her out of the shower then and dry her off. Lila brought us clothes and helped us dress. When we got out to the main room Lila had hot chocolate waiting for us. We sat and sipped in silence for a long time. Finally we all three went to bed, Clara cuddled between us in case she woke up with nightmares. Dog lay at the foot of the bed and kept watch as we slept.

A couple of weeks later Clara got back to work. It had taken some major strings and most of the favors Sam and I both had to buy CLara that much time to recover. She's seeing a therapist and is making progress. I didn't think a therapist was a good idea but Lila knew a witch who was clued in enough to be safe and who was a mental health practitioner.

I thought about attending myself but then just couldn't do it. Which was probably stupid since I could guarantee I needed therapy more than anyone. But anyone who had dated my former girlfriend who worked in mental health would have major trust issues as well.

Lila presented me with two gifts of thanks for killing Marcus. The first was a beautiful sword she had commissioned for me. It had the flexibility of a falchion and the shape and length of a katana. It was truly a work of art.

The second came in a rosewood box. She met me for dinner and brought it along. Inside the box was the sole deed for Heller and all its subsidiaries. Apparently she had been working to grow Heller as a business and it was doing really well. She said she thought I had earned it having spent so many years growing Heller as an entity. She told me the loft and office were still hers, but that she'd share them with me.

She also got Dog a flexible armored vest similar to what our K9's wear in the field. I thought he would intimidate bullets into going the other way, but he liked it. I still didn't know what to do about the job Major Murphy had offered me. There hadn't been any more snooping alphabet soup boys but I knew they'd be back sometime. Uncle Sugar never lets you get away clean.

And as for me personally, I felt like I was whole again. I was certainly a different person, but hopefully I was a better man than I had been before. Perhaps I had found my personal redemption. I hadn't had any of the nightmares since the night I killed Marcus, so maybe I had let the dead go to their graves after all. It was a good feeling to be free, and to know that others were safe because of my actions. It almost felt like I was helping people again. And that was really important to me. I only had one problem left. What was I going to name Dog?

Don't miss out!

Visit the website below and you can sign up to receive emails whenever Charles M. Brown publishes a new book. There's no charge and no obligation.

https://books2read.com/r/B-A-HOQMC-MJUID

BOOKS 2 READ

Connecting independent readers to independent writers.

Did you love *Nihil*? Then you should read *Gaeth's Redemption*[1] by Charles M. Brown!

[2]

"You always warned me that being queen would mean my death." - Simone

A romantic war story that starts when Gaeth a man with a war-torn heart, meets Simone a woman too afraid to become queen. With losses accrued on both sides, the couple struggles to find a balance between the magical chemistry within them and the catastrophic destiny that awaits them. Gathe's Redemption features yokai, witches, descriptive

---

1. https://books2read.com/u/4EB7Gg

2. https://books2read.com/u/4EB7Gg

battles, and some spicey scenes all coming together to show that the lines of war and lust are not all that different.

Read more at https://www.hellhoundsrun.com/.